Once
There Were
Mermaids

Once There Were Mermaids

CAROL ANN MARTIN

An Omnibus Book from Scholastic Australia

LEXILE™ 880

Omnibus Books
335 Unley Road, Malvern SA 5061
an imprint of Scholastic Australia Pty Ltd (ABN 11 000 614 577)
PO Box 579, Gosford NSW 2250.
www.scholastic.com.au

Part of the Scholastic Group
Sydney · Auckland · New York · Toronto · London · Mexico City ·
New Delhi · Hong Kong · Buenos Aires · Puerto Rico

First published in 2005.
Text copyright © Carol Ann Martin, 2005.

National Library of Australia Cataloguing-in-Publication entry
Martin, Ann, 1942–   .
Once there were mermaids.
ISBN 1 86291 625 X.
I. Title.
A823.3

Typeset in 12.5/17.5 pt Perpetua by Clinton Ellicott, Adelaide.
Printed in Australia by McPherson's Printing Group, Maryborough, Victoria.

10 9 8 7 6 5 4 3 2 1   5 6 7 8 9 / 0

For everyone who has ever been dump

Dear Mr McDewey,

I am writing to you about the Hughey McDewey Super Chewy Toffee Junior Writing Award. I know I'm supposed to send in an entry form, but I thought a letter would be better. There's a lot of stuff you need to know.

I am nearly fourteen years old and I have written heaps of books. I really hope I can win your award. It's not just the $200, even though we could do with it. What I want is my story published in *Kidscene*, like you said. After that it should be a cinch to get all my other stuff published too.

My dad says the award is a gimmick to get people to buy your toffee. If that's true, it is Good Thinking, Mr McDewey. I guess that's why you want six Super Chewy wrappers sent in with every entry. If mine smell a bit funny, it's because I had to get them out of a rubbish bin.

I think your toffee is great. But for personal reasons I am not able to eat it.

You will be interested to know that the story I have written is a true one. It happened to a girl I know. She has poured her heart and soul and all her innermost secrets out to me. And she said it would be OK for me to enter her story in your competition.

This girl is named Miranda Hodge. Her nickname is Podge, which is quite cruel really. But it gets worse. When Miranda has to wear her sports shorts, she gets 'Hippo-Bum'. It was Jacinta Jacques who started that one.

Anyway, what happened was that last summer Miranda spent the holidays with her ex-half-sister-in-law. That sounds complicated, but I will explain.

Miranda's dad is named Brian. Back in the seventies, when he wasn't her dad yet, he was going to be a rock star. I guess that to have your own toffee factory you have to be pretty old. So you probably remember Elvis Presley. I don't remember him, but I've seen him on videos. Elvis was the King of Rock. But by 1973 he'd got fat, and he wasn't doing very much.

Brian Hodge was only twenty-two and dead skinny. He reckoned he'd got what it took to be the next King. For a start, he had an electric guitar. He also had hair that flopped in his eyes and totally cool tight black pants with sequins on them. When he sang, he wriggled and twitched as though he had bull ants in his pants. (I'm not making this up. Miranda has seen photos.)

Quite a few girls at that time thought that Brian was even groovier than Elvis. One of them was named Celandine Ambrazine. Please take note of the name Ambrazine. You are going to hear it a lot.

Here are a few ways you can recognise an Ambrazine if you meet one.

All Ambrazines are super good-looking.

All Ambrazines are mega-rich.

All Ambrazines are absolute stinkers.

Anyway, this Ambrazine called Celandine had made up her mind. If Brian was going to be the next King of Rock, she was going to be his Queen. She had the long blonde hair for it, and the long legs and the little skinny frocks. All she needed were a few photo opportunities and she'd be in every magazine on earth. Celandine reckoned that Brian's hit records would take care of that. So she ran away with him and married him. This made her parents go seriously ballistic. But Celandine didn't care.

A year later Brian and Celandine had a baby boy. Celandine named him Magnus Ambrazine Hodge. By that time Brian should have been at the top of the charts. But he wasn't. He wasn't exactly in the charts at all. He hadn't even exactly made a record yet. But he was still hoping. While he was waiting to become famous he was working as a builder's labourer and singing in pubs on Saturday nights.

'Believe in me, Celandine,' he said. 'Trust me, and we'll be right.'

But Celandine said, 'No way, José!', which was seventies for 'In your dreams!' And with that she dumped him. Naturally that pleased her parents no end. Ambrazines love to see people dumped. They welcomed Celandine and Magnus into their home and bought a rottweiler to keep Brian away.

Celandine chopped the Hodge bit off Magnus's name and did her best to chop Brian out of his life. But then she found herself a new husband. Actually she found three in a row, each one richer than the one before. All this getting married and divorced kept Celandine pretty busy, so when Magnus was six she put him in a boarding school. But because she kept forgetting when the terms ended, the school always sent Magnus to Brian for the holidays.

By this time Brian was a qualified builder. It was easier than being the King of Rock, and he was better at it. For a long time it seemed as though Celandine had put him right off marriage. But when he was quite old, about thirty-five, he met Judy Kelly.

Judy was a childcare nurse, and she made hot chocolate to die for. She was ten years younger than Brian, but she was fabulously big and soft and squidgy.

At the clinic where Judy worked, a baby could be screaming itself rigid and going purple in the face. But the minute Judy picked that baby up, it would burrow itself into her cushiony front, wipe its nose all over her uniform, snuffle happily, and fall sound asleep. Judy had that effect on people.

By the time Brian had finished building a new kitchen at the clinic, she had had that effect on him. He had found the second Mrs Hodge.

So Judy recycled Celandine's cast-off husband, and with lots of hugs and hot chocolate she fixed him up as good as new. In the school holidays she gave great dollops of love to Celandine's dumped son, Magnus. He slurped it all up, of course. But from his yellow-tipped hair to the soles of his top-of-the-range runners, he was still an absolute Ambrazine.

When Judy had a baby girl of her own, she named her Kelly, after herself. Four years later she had another girl. This one she named Miranda, because she liked the name.

So Miranda had a much older half-brother who was more like a rich, good-looking uncle dropping in and out of her life. Then, when Miranda was nine, Magnus married a girl named Blossom Bunting. Two years later he dumped her, because that's what Ambrazines do. But the Hodges all liked Blossom and they stayed good friends with her.

That's how Miranda came to have an ex-half-sister-in-law. I told you there was stuff you needed to know. The rest is in the story.

Thank you for your time. I trust that this letter finds you in good health.

Yours very truly,

Tallulah Hopewell (Ms)

Chapter 1

Alone on the hilltop, horse and rider stood silhouetted against the crimson sky. Theodelinda gazed out across the plain to where the last of her foes lay on the blood-soaked ground, or staggered brokenly into the forest beyond.

With slender hands she reached up and pulled the war helmet from her head. Like a glistening mountain stream, her silken hair cascaded down over her slim shoulders. Caught by the rays of the setting sun, the tresses shimmered a deep red-gold. Arrow-straight she sat, her grey-green, long-lashed eyes victorious yet serene.

'We have won, Starlight,' she whispered huskily to her faithful silver steed. 'Victory is ours.'

Then, with a flashing smile, she rode down the hillside towards whatever the future held.

Miranda slid onto her back, closed the book and laid it on her stomach.

Was this really the end? After so many enthralling weeks

with Theodelinda, Warrior Princess of the Celts, was the story finally over?

No, she decided, it couldn't be. Returning to her scrunched-up position against the pillows, she opened the book again and picked up her pen. 'Chapter 37' she wrote at the top of the next clean page.

Ten minutes later, that was as far as she'd got. Miranda was having a serious attack of Writer's Block. Flat on her back again, she stared at the cracks in her bedroom ceiling and tried not to cry. That's what Writer's Block does to you. Your imagination jams up like a bicycle wheel with the chain stuck and you just want to burst into tears.

Miranda had a father who could fix blocked toilets, sinks and drains. She had a mother who could fix blocked ears, noses and just about any other part of the human body. But only one person in the world could fix Miranda's Writer's Block.

Flopping over the edge of the bed, she groped underneath it and found a thick paperback book: *Quest for the Golden Girdle, Volume Four of the Tressellyn Chronicles*, by Rhiannon Fayn.

Miranda rubbed the glossy cover like Aladdin rubbing his lamp. Then she turned the book over and gazed at the photograph on the back.

Had anyone ever called Rhiannon Fayn 'Hippo-Bum'? Did Rhiannon Fayn have legs so fat at the top that they rubbed together and gave her a rash in hot weather? Had the red silk dress that Rhiannon Fayn wore come from a jumble sale? Miranda didn't think so.

Rhiannon Fayn had crinkly blonde hair that rippled down each side of her pale, narrow face. Her eyes were cool and grey and mysterious, almost as mysterious as the smile that gently curved her lips. And Rhiannon Fayn wrote the most totally fabulous books that Miranda had ever read.

She yearned to visit Miss Fayn's website. But the Hodges weren't on the Net, so Miranda had written her a letter at her publisher's address. She had told Miss Fayn how much she adored the Tressellyn Chronicles, and explained that she, Miranda, wrote stories very much like that herself. Now she was waiting for a reply.

In the meantime, just holding the paperback worked like a magic charm. She felt the power whizzing out of the pages, up her arms and into her brain. Unblocked at last, she began to scribble as fast as she could to keep up with the rush of words.

It was a sudden burst of wind that told Theodelinda that Lord Finnewulf drew nigh. The elements were always her messengers and she listened now with beating heart. He had returned, as he had vowed he would, the bold young chieftain from afar. With his wild dark hair and flashing dark eyes, soon he would be at her door.

She heard hoofbeats across the courtyard. Nimble feet leaped lightly up the stair. A gauntleted hand threw the portal wide and at last she heard his voice . . .

'Hey Podge! Do you *have* to lie around like a lazy lump of lard? Get out here and give me a hand!'

Miranda blinked groggily as reality dawned. Her parents had gone out, she'd forgotten where, and Kelly was making dinner. With a sigh, she slid off the bed.

On her way to the door she stopped and looked hopefully in her mirror. But she didn't seem to be any paler or narrower than she'd been the last time she'd looked. The best thing about her was still her long hair, which was the colour of Hughey McDewey's Super Chewy Toffee. She wore it with a centre parting, just like Rhiannon Fayn. But Miranda's hair neither crinkled nor rippled down each side of her face. It just hung there, so that her face looked like a full moon shining between a pair of curtains.

She tried a flashing smile, but the only thing that flashed was the wire braces on her teeth. So she went for a mysterious smile, which she could do without opening her mouth. And with that firmly fixed on her lips, she went to find out what Kelly was making for dinner.

Chapter 2

Kelly was in the kitchen with her bottom sticking out of the fridge. It was a bottom that Miranda would have liked for herself. But Kelly was tall and slim like Brian, and Miranda was short and round like Judy. No way was that going to change.

Kelly's rear end was decorated with big red satin love hearts. She was doing dress design at college and was right into love hearts just now. They looked super cool on the catsuit she had made out of an op shop leotard.

'Hiya, Slob-Podge!' Kelly turned round with an armful of pots, jars and plastic containers and kicked the fridge door shut with her foot. The slam woke a ratty-haired, mangy old dog that was lying across the back door. It opened bloodshot eyes and bared its yellow teeth in a snarl.

'Rack off, Poo-face!' said Kelly, dumping her armload on the table. 'Bog in,' she told Miranda. 'It's catch and kill your own tonight.'

Miranda scooped up a scabby, scar-faced cat that was licking the margarine. It hissed and writhed in her hands, looking for a good spot to sink in its claws. She tossed it at the dog, who snarled again, while the cat seemed to have some kind of fit in mid-air.

'You going out?' she asked Kelly.

With her hair glued sideways in streaks across her face, thick black rings around her eyes and purple lipstick, her sister did look as though she might be about to hit the town.

'Nah.' Kelly poured tomato sauce over a bowl of cold spaghetti. 'They wouldn't let me. I've got to mind you.'

Ever since Miranda had turned thirteen she'd been trying to convince Judy that she didn't need a minder. So far she hadn't succeeded. But Miranda knew that Kelly didn't mind minding her. And Miranda didn't mind too much being minded by Kelly. To tell the truth, her sister was the closest thing she had to a best friend.

'Where've they gone?' she asked through a mouthful of tuna quiche.

'HoHo!' said Kelly. 'Where else?'

HoHo was what Brian and Judy did. It was their work. HoHo stood for 'Hands-On Help Organisation', a bunch of people who went around doing helpful stuff for other people who couldn't do it for themselves. Brian mostly built things and fixed things that were broken. Judy mostly told mums without much money that fruit and vegies were heaps better for their kids than icypoles and chips. HoHoing didn't pay a lot, which was why the Hodges never had much money.

The trouble with Judy was that HoHoing wasn't just her job, it was her life. The mangy dog and the scabby cat were both strays that she'd brought in off the street. 'All they need is love,' she said. She was still saying it after five stitches and a tetanus jab for dog bites, and a lounge suite that permanently ponged of cat piddle.

The girls really liked times like now, with nothing to do but eat custard straight out of the carton and talk about movie stars who would one day wear clothes that Kelly had designed in movies that Miranda had written. And that's what they were doing at half past eight, when Brian and Judy got home.

The first thing Judy did was to get out the saucepan for hot chocolate. Miranda could feel something big coming on, and she wasn't wrong.

HoHo was going overseas. Not all of it, but a team, and Brian and Judy were on it. Somewhere up in the highlands of Papua New Guinea a little village was about to be HoHoed whether it liked it or not. Brian was going to help build them a baby health clinic and Judy was going to show them what to do with it.

They sat round the table and the girls let their hot chocolate go cold while all that sank in.

Then, 'I'm not going!' said Kelly.

'Too right you're not,' said Brian. And then they were told what was going to happen to them.

Cynthia Truscott, a HoHo whose main job was knitting socks, was coming to housesit. But Cynthia only sat houses, pets and pot plants, not people. So Kelly and Miranda were going to stay with Granny Hodge.

'I could stay at Melanie's! I know I could!' Kelly was getting excited about the possibilities of a whole month without her parents around.

Miranda wasn't excited. It was just another big bummer in her life. Kelly would get to stay with her best friend, and Miranda would stay by herself with Granny Hodge. And that would be *so* boring. Why did things like this always happen to her?

Chapter 3

Not everything worked out the way Miranda thought it would.
The bit about Kelly being allowed to stay at Melanie's place did.
But the bit about Granny Hodge didn't.

Granny's bowls team, the Under Eighties Mean Machine,
won their grand finals. That meant they got to go on a three-
week bowling tour of New Zealand in January. So Granny
wouldn't be around to look after Miranda.

'Well, that's it,' said Brian. 'We don't go to New Guinea.'

'You've got to go!' howled Kelly. 'I've made my plans!'

Like Judy, Kelly was a person with a lot of love to give.
Right now she was giving most of it to a guy at college named
Bronson, who had a ponytail and wrote poetry. Kelly wasn't
supposed to be going with Bronson, because he wrote words in
his poetry that people usually only write on the walls of bus
shelters and public toilets. Kelly said that great poetry was
meant to shock. Brian said that in that case some of the world's

greatest poets had worked on his building sites, and no daughter of his was going out with a bloke who used language like that. But with Brian and Judy off to New Guinea . . . Except that they weren't now, were they?

Nobody, not even Kelly, actually said it was all Miranda's fault because she didn't have a best friend to stay with. So Miranda didn't have to explain that at the school she went to, if you were fat and not especially pretty and your uniform was second-hand, best friends were hard to come by. But it was a fact. Just the same as it was a fact that some things in life can't be fixed with hugs and hot chocolate.

Then, a couple of mornings later, something truly awesome happened. Jacinta Jacques and Amy Bakewell had a fight at school. That wasn't the awesome thing, it happened all the time. Jacinta had only picked Amy for her best friend so that she could turn mean on her and make her cry any time she wanted to. Miranda sometimes wondered if there wasn't some Ambrazine blood in Jacinta somewhere.

Only this time Amy didn't cry. Instead she came up to Miranda at recess and offered her a Hughey McDewey Super Chewy Toffee.

'I can't,' said Miranda. 'It'll get stuck in my braces.'

Jacinta pretended to be just passing by, but Miranda could see she was having a good stickybeak. Amy looked sideways at Jacinta and then put her arm around Miranda's shoulders.

'Are you going anywhere in the holidays?' she asked.

Miranda shook her head, too amazed by all this friendliness to answer.

'We're going to my uncle's farm in the Riverina,' said Amy. 'Mum says I can bring a friend. D'you want to come?'

Miranda nodded, but she couldn't believe it. She went on not being able to believe it until Mrs Bakewell rang up that night and asked proper permission for Miranda to go on holiday with them.

'You little ripper beauty!' This time it was Kelly who hugged her.

Judy and Brian very kindly didn't carry on as if a miracle had happened. But Judy did make super deluxe hot chocolate with marshmallows on top.

Miranda went to bed that night truly, deeply, madly happy. She was going to stay on a farm with Amy, who obviously wanted her for a friend. And not only that, everybody else could go where they wanted to go, because they didn't have to worry about her.

The next morning, the first thing Miranda saw when she walked through the school gates was Jacinta and Amy. They had their arms round each other and their heads were close together.

Jacinta looked across and saw Miranda. Then Amy looked too.

Whisper, whisper, and Jacinta gave Amy a little push. Amy started to walk towards Miranda, and Jacinta walked a few steps behind. Miranda started to get a hot, lurching feeling in her stomach.

Amy stopped in front of her. She didn't look at Miranda's face, but at her sandals. 'Look,' she said. 'That holiday thing . . . Jacinta's dad is hiring a yacht. They're going to the Barrier Reef, and . . . Jacinta . . . Jacinta . . . asked . . .'

The hot, lurching feeling had moved up into Miranda's chest and her legs began to wobble.

You can't not . . . go on a yacht. The words were rolling round in her head like a stupid little poem, but her throat was too tight to let her say it.

'So I guess we won't be going to the farm,' Amy was finishing up. 'Perhaps at Easter, hey?'

Miranda looked at Jacinta, and Jacinta was smiling. It was a glittery little smile that said, *I win*.

'Sure, Easter.' Miranda sat down on a bench and looked straight ahead. Anywhere but at Jacinta's smile.

There was a thunder of hoofs across the playgound. Even at full gallop Theodelinda was poised with perfect grace upon her steed. Her slender arms held aloft a mighty double-edged sword. Supple as a willow wand, she bent from the saddle and with one swipe of the sword she sliced off Jacinta's head.

The head, not smiling now, but grotesque with terror, bounced along the ground in a thick trail of blood.

Miranda shuddered. This was a bit over the top, even for Theodelinda. So she put Jacinta's head back on her shoulders and the smile back on her face. Then she looked Jacinta straight in the eyes.

'It's cool,' she said. 'I'm allergic to cows anyway.' And on legs that still wobbled, she got up and walked away.

But it wasn't cool. She'd been dumped. And it really, really hurt.

That night Mrs Bakewell rang again. This time it was to say how sorry she was that the holiday plans had been changed. Brian took the call.

'That's all right, Mrs Bakewell,' he said. 'Matter of fact, it's all turned out for the best. Me and Mrs Hodge, we're a bit fussy about who our girls mix with. We try to teach them loyalty, integrity, stuff like that. Doesn't seem like Miranda'd learn much of that from you lot, would she?'

'You tell 'em, Dad!' Kelly cheered as Brian slammed down the phone.

But Miranda just sat down on the cat-piddled sofa and howled. Judy sat beside her and tried to take her in her arms.

'It's no good, Mum,' Miranda sobbed. 'I'm a reject. A loser! A total waste of space!' And that was enough to start Judy crying too.

Fat black mascara tears started rolling down Kelly's face. She gnawed her fingernails and muttered, 'Far out!' while Brian handed round tissues. It was the worst night ever.

Then the phone rang again. Brian was the only one in a fit state to answer it, and he seemed quite pleased that he had.

'It's Blossom,' he said, holding the phone out to Judy.

Judy blew her nose and took the phone. 'Hi, sweetie . . . No, no, just getting a cold, I think. How are you doing?'

How Blossom was doing took a long time to tell. At first Judy just made polite 'Oh' and 'Right' noises. Then she gave out a great big knocked-for-six 'Oh!' for real. Her eyes got rounder and rounder, and everybody stopped crying and nail-gnawing and listened.

If they hadn't known it was Blossom they would have thought it was the Red Cross ringing up to tell Judy she'd won the five-speed four-wheel-drive with power steering, alloy wheels, electronic windows and air conditioning valued at $39,000 in their raffle.

At last Judy blurted, 'Well, I think Kelly's got plans. But Miranda . . .' A huge smile started to spread across her face. 'Hang on! I'll put her on.'

20

She waggled the phone at Miranda and mouthed, *Yes! Yes! Yes!*

'Somebody else getting a cold?' asked Blossom, as Miranda croaked tearily down the phone.

It was good to hear Blossom's chirrupy voice, which always sounded as though she was about twelve years old instead of twice that. 'Hey, Mim! Guess what! I've got this place in Tasmania. It's at Mariners Bay, right on the beach, and I've turned it into a café. I've got a life, Mim! A whole new life!'

Miranda, who hadn't got a life, said, 'Cool', and tried to mean it. But Blossom hadn't finished yet. 'I want you guys to see it. Judy says Kelly's got stuff to do this summer. But you can come, can't you, Mim? Go on, say you'll come!'

Miranda leaned against the wall. Her legs were wobbling again, and more tears were gushing up. *Sucked in, Jacinta Jacques. Sucked in, Amy Bakewell. Sucked in, anybody who thought Miranda Hodge had nowhere to go. Thank you, Blossom. I love you, Blossom.*

'Sure,' she said. 'I'll come.'

Chapter 4

As soon as Christmas was over, the Hodges were off. Miranda was the first to go. She was booked to fly to Hobart on the morning of December the twenty-ninth.

'Big deal!' Jacinta had said when Miranda had casually mentioned that fact just before school broke up. 'I've been flying by myself since I was six!' What Miranda had decided not to mention was that Judy had rung the airline and asked that her daughter should travel as an *unaccompanied minor*, which meant she had to have a minder yet again.

Miranda had thought that going to the airport would be dead scary. But it was utterly embarrassing instead.

Nobody else had a pink plastic suitcase held together with a dog lead. Nobody else had a sister in a red mini Santa frock with a white fluffy boa and black fishnet stockings. Nobody else had a mother who kept clutching her, crying all over her, and asking her if she wanted to go to the toilet one last time.

So when her minder, a flight attendant drop-dead gorgeous enough to be Lord Finnewulf, said it was time to take her aboard, she was out of there in a flash.

Once the plane was up in the air, it all got scary again. Miranda's fingers felt like frozen sausages when she tried to unwrap the muesli and orange juice that Lord Finnewulf brought to her sealed in plastic. Then she found that she didn't want them anyway, so she closed her eyes and made up a story about an airline that lost little Jacinta and didn't find her again for thirty years.

Then, as sometimes happened, someone turned up in her mind and wanted to be in a Theodelinda story. This time it was a dark, statuesque woman dressed all in black. She had raven hair streaked with silver and heavy-lidded eyes in a strong and noble face. She even arrived with a name, which was always a help. It was Glamorga, Goddess of High Mountain Places. Miranda knew she ought to write her down. But her notebook was in her suitcase, and Lord Finnewulf was checking that her seatbelt was fastened for landing.

Safely on the ground in Hobart, he delivered her into the airport lounge. But who was he delivering her to? Miranda could only gape at the figure that rushed towards her. It was someone in a floppy brown swagman's hat decorated with black feathers. The top half wore a shrunken yellow top that showed a belly button with a ring in it, and the bottom half was wrapped in what looked like part of an old bedspread. All this was finished off with a pair of bushwalking boots without laces.

But whoever it was sounded like Blossom. It was Blossom's driving licence that the flight attendant had to look at before he handed Miranda over. And it was Blossom's little freckled face under the hat when at last they got to squeal and hug and kiss.

What had happened to Blossom? Why was she dressed in rags? Miranda could only think that Magnus had left her without a cent to her name. It would be an Ambrazine thing to do.

If he had, Blossom didn't seem to care. She bubbled and burbled the way she always did while she took Miranda out to the car park and to the biggest heap of junk Miranda had ever seen.

It was hard to tell what was holding Blossom's purple-and-pink Kombi together. Probably the mud, and the stickers all over it that said NO WAR, NO LOGGING, NO DAMS, GREEN IS BEAUTIFUL, and, more interestingly, MAGIC HAPPENS. And this was the girl who used to drive a white Italian sports car!

It was a long drive down to Mariners Bay, and on the way Miranda learned a lot of things. For a start her ex-half-sister-in-law had become a black swan. And that wasn't an all-girl footy team either.

'Everything in creation is connected,' Blossom told her. 'Us, the trees, the sky, the sea, the birds, the animals, the whole box of tricks. And we have each other's spirits in us. I've got the spirit of a black swan. I wonder what yours is.'

Miranda hadn't a clue, but the words 'Hippo-Bum' came into her head. She wasn't sure about Blossom being a swan either. A ginger kitten would have been more like it.

The next thing she learned was that Magnus hadn't left Blossom without any money. He was throwing it at her with both hands and she was throwing it right back. 'Who needs his lousy money?' she said. And she told Miranda what Magnus could do with it. But it sounded pretty gross and not really an Ambrazine thing.

Then Miranda heard something that took a bit of the shine off the day. With her own money, just about all of it, Blossom had indeed bought an old wooden house at Mariners Bay. She'd turned it into a café, and now she needed some help with it.

'That's where you come in, Mim,' she said.

Miranda's heart went clunk. So that was it. She was here to HoHo in the kitchen all summer. Wash those dishes! Mop that floor! Ripped off, dumped on again. And by Blossom of all people.

They came to a town that Blossom said had no soul. But it did have public loos, so they stopped for a minute or two.

'See what I mean?' Blossom asked as they drove on. 'That town doesn't have any vibes whatsoever.'

25

By now the road was getting rougher, and the Kombi was providing all the vibes Miranda could handle. It was a nice view, though: bushland and paddocks on one side and flashes of sparkling sea through the trees on the other. Miranda tried not to think about the piles of dirty dishes waiting for her at the end of the journey.

Then Blossom swung onto an even rougher road and all Miranda could do was hold on to her seatbelt and wait for the Kombi to fall apart around them. But somehow it hung together, and in about ten minutes they arrived at another town, sort of.

Blossom didn't say if that one had a soul, but Miranda thought it might have been too small for one. All she could see was a shop, a petrol pump, about ten houses and what looked like a little church. There were no people, but a dead dog lay in the middle of the road.

Over the door of the shop was a sign that said: MARINERS BAY SUPERMARKET, POST OFFICE, NEWSAGENCY AND LIBRARY. *S. Konopolous, Prop*. Whatever was inside couldn't be seen from the outside because of all the bits of paper stickytaped to the window and MERRY CHRISTMAS sprayed in Santa snow.

Blossom didn't exactly park there. She just stopped. 'Come on,' she said. 'We have to check the mail.'

Trying not to look at the dead dog, Miranda followed Blossom into the Mariners Bay supermarket, post office, newsagency and library.

Just inside the door they were nearly run over by a little old lady with a shopping trolley. She was snowy-haired, apple-cheeked and dangerous. As she swerved to miss them she almost took out a display of Hughey McDewey's Super Chewy Toffees.

'They are the work of the devil!' she cried in a voice with a lot of rolling rrrs. Miranda guessed that she meant shopping trolleys and not toffees. 'I shall not be defeated!' the old lady assured them, and she ran the trolley over Blossom's foot.

Miranda did her best to escape, but another wild swing of the trolley had her pinned against the cornflakes.

Trapped, cornered, Theodelinda lifted her softly curved yet resolute chin. With steady eyes she confronted her captor. The Warrior Princess would die before she would surrender. With every nerve tensed for action, she watched for the next move. Watched the hand that stealthily crept forth . . .

The old woman pulled a big patchwork handbag out of the trolley and delved inside it until she found a matching spectacles case. She put the spectacles on and looked Miranda up and down.

'You're Blossom's sister-in-law from Sydney,' she said.

Miranda wondered if she should thank her for that valuable piece of information. Instead, she gave her a smile – the mysterious one that didn't show her braces.

'Right, Mrs Lovelace,' said Blossom. 'I just got her from the airport.'

Mrs Lovelace gave Miranda another close look.

'She seems a big, strong girl,' she said.

Miranda's heart went clunk again. In *The Quest for the Golden Girdle* Lady Alyce had said exactly the same thing about her new serving wench.

Mrs Lovelace's bright blue gaze went on and on, as if she'd never seen anyone quite like Miranda before. In the end it was Blossom who got the trolley into reverse and helped Mrs Lovelace wrestle it through the door. The old lady was still looking back over her shoulder.

Then something very weird happened.

Down the aisle, between the soap powder and the dog biscuits, glided the Goddess Glamorga, her black silky dress whispering like a spell.

'You are Blossom's sister-in-law from Sydney,' the goddess announced in a deep, husky voice.

Miranda forgot about her braces and let her mouth drop open. What was Glamorga doing in the Mariners Bay super-market? Miranda hadn't even written her down yet.

Blossom had got Mrs Lovelace safely out at last. Now she was acting as though she talked with goddesses every day.

'Mim,' she said, 'this is Sofie Konopolous, our shopkeeper, postmistress and librarian.' Not a word about her being Goddess of High Mountain Places.

The goddess turned her burning gaze to Blossom. 'That is a horrible hat,' she said. 'Why do you hide such a pretty face under such an ugly hat?'

Blossom laughed. 'Any mail for me?' she asked.

With more swishing of her skirts, the goddess led them to the back of the shop. Miranda thought this was a funny place to keep the checkout, but then she saw that it was a post office counter as well. There were pigeonholes all along the wall, and a doorway with one of those curtains made of coloured plastic strips. Miranda supposed that behind the plastic was where the goddess lived.

Glamorga took an envelope out of one of the pigeonholes. 'Another cheque from him,' she said.

'Send it back,' said Blossom.

The goddess shrugged her shoulders and tossed the envelope into a wire basket.

'Throw away that hat,' she said. 'Burn it. I have a hat I will give you.' She twirled her hands around her own piled-up hairdo. 'It is white, with a little what-do-you-call-it. Very pretty.'

Miranda was losing count of the number of times today that things hadn't been what they'd seemed. This was no goddess. A goddess wouldn't be yakking on about hats. She wouldn't be telling Blossom that somebody had bought the great big Robinson place on the headland, and ooh, aah, how much had they paid for it? She might look like Glamorga, but she really was Sofie Thingummy. And all this gasbagging was so boring.

So Miranda went for a wander round the shop. That told her a lot. People here went for sheep dip, chook pellets and mouse-traps in a big way. Christmas puddings were now half price. The local newspaper was called the *Southern Bugle*, and magazines about cows, fortune-telling and tractors were very popular. There was no sign of the library. Mariners Bay had probably never even heard of Rhiannon Fayn.

She wandered outside and started reading the notices in the window.

Don't miss the Grand Finals of the Sheep Shearing Contest.

For Sale. Thirty metres of pre-loved barbed wire.

Lost. The little round rubber bit off the end of my walking stick.

Miranda didn't know if she could handle all the excitement in Mariners Bay.

The next second a hoon on a bicycle came at her from nowhere, swerved, and missed her by centimetres.

'Maniac!' she called after him. What was it about this town and mowing people down? Was there a prize for the last one left standing?

The hoon gave her a really rude finger gesture. Then he chucked a U-ey round the dead dog and reared up onto his back wheel.

The dog couldn't have been dead after all, because it leaped up and went for the bike. The bike crashed over backwards and the dog ran yelping down the street.

Miranda ran towards the tangled heap of spinning wheels and flapping legs. She clearly heard some words straight out of one of Bronson's poems, so the idiot under the bike wasn't too badly hurt.

'You all right?' she asked, reaching out her hand in case he needed it.

'Don't touch me!' snarled a voice. 'Nobody touches the Mangler!'

Miranda backed off. 'Who'd want to?' she asked. But all the same, she watched him stagger to his feet.

He was an amazingly tall and skinny boy dressed all in black. The design on the front of his singlet top showed a hatchet dripping blood, and it looked as though he could have painted it on himself. Both his elbows were also dripping blood.

'You ought to get those fixed,' she told him.

'Butt out, you!' he answered. Then he took off his crash hat, and Miranda could only stare again.

If this guy was into Blossom's spirit thing, then he just had to be an emu. Beady black eyes glowered from each side of a beaky nose. And the head on top of the long scrawny neck was totally bald.

'Whatcher staring at?' he asked.

'You tell me,' said Miranda. 'Did you say you were the Strangler?'

'Mangler,' he growled. 'Get it right.' Then he said, in a really up-himself voice, 'Anyway, I know who you are.'

That'd be right, thought Miranda. The whole town knew who she was. But all of a sudden she didn't feel like hearing Emu Features tell her she was Blossom's sister-in-law from Sydney.

'As a matter of fact,' she said, 'I happen to be a Celtic Warrior Princess.'

'Well, *excuse me!*' he said. '*I* just happen to be Mangler Malone, streetfighter, exterminator, and numero uno Melbourne gangleader!'

'Bull!' said Miranda.

'Well, you'd know, wouldn't you?' he sneered. 'You being a fairy princess and all that.'

'Celtic princess!' she snapped.

'Celtic fruitloop!' he snapped back.

'Pelican-poop-brain!' Miranda had never yelled abuse in the street before, and she was surprised to find that she was good at it.

'Constipated camel face!' The boy wasn't bad, either.

'Cut it out, you two!' Blossom came belting out of the supermarket in a little white satin hat with a spotted veil. Close behind her came Sofie, bellowing, 'We will not have this shouting!' Then she saw the bleeding elbows, and she let out a scream that rattled windows.

The boy threw up his hands. 'It's OK, it's OK!' he said. For an experienced streetfighter he seemed to give up very easily. 'I came off my bike, that's all.'

Miranda expected to see smoke coming out of Sofie's nostrils. 'Showing off!' she hissed. 'Always showing off!'

Obviously she didn't know that it's politically incorrect to grab somebody by the ear and pull, because next moment the boy's head was yanked down so that Blossom could get a close-up.

'See what he did?' Sofie said. 'His beautiful curls, all gone.'

Blossom said she quite liked it, but Sofie was close to tears. 'He will break his poor mother's heart,' she said.

'What heart?' asked the boy, once his head was back up where it belonged.

'Ah, come on, Nigel,' said Blossom.

Nigel? Miranda couldn't help grinning, even if it did show her braces. '*Nigel* Mangler Malone?'

Sofie frowned. 'Who said mangle? He is Nygel Featherstone. And that is Nygel with a Y.'

Miranda felt her grin spreading. 'With a Y? Why a Y?'

Nygel gave her a filthy scowl. 'You got a problem with a Y?'

Before Miranda could answer, Blossom grabbed her arm. 'I'll be the one with problems if we don't get going,' she said quickly.

Sofie gave Nygel a shove. 'You! Inside!' And inside he slouched, while she snapped at his heels like a sheepdog. 'And take off that shirt. Why would a nice boy wear such a shirt? You will break your poor mother's heart!'

Miranda didn't think her own mother would have been too impressed either, not by all that yobbish yelling from her daughter.

34

'Sorry,' she said to Blossom as they climbed aboard the Kombi. 'But he *is* a total nerd.'

Blossom smiled. 'Ah, Nygel isn't so bad,' she said. And she drove carefully around the fake dead dog, which had come back to lie in the road next to Nygel's bike.

Chapter 6

The trouble with being a writer is that stuff comes into your head and you can't get it out again. As the Kombi rattled back onto the coast road, Nygel Featherstone was the last thing Miranda wanted to think about. Nygel Featherstone was a total waste of space, especially in somebody's head. But he wouldn't quit, and neither would his mother.

She was a thin, frail woman with tragic eyes in a white, haggard face. And she was slowly dying of a broken heart because her son was such a moron.

And another thing. Who was Sofie Whatsit? And what was the strange power she had over Nygel? Miranda asked Blossom.

'She's his nanny,' Blossom told her. 'A sort of minder he gets sent to when his mother goes away.'

So Nygel had minders too. Miranda wondered if the members of the Mangler's gang knew that their fearless leader had a nanny.

Blossom parked the Kombi on a sandy crescent at the side of the road. 'We're here,' she said. 'The rest is on foot.'

Miranda saw a rainbow-coloured sign that said COSMOS CAFÉ, and an arrow pointing to a path between the trees. She got out of the Kombi and looked over the edge of a steep bushy slope. And every thought of Nygel, his mother and his nanny went clean out of her head.

It wasn't just the sea, shining in every shade of green and turquoise and blue. It wasn't just the smooth, scalloped, creamy-coloured cliffs. And it wasn't just the dark, rolling hills beyond, holding the bay in the curve of their arms. It was a really deep, and really *real*, feeling that this was her own special place. It had been waiting for her forever.

Blossom stood beside her and pointed down into the bay. Miranda looked, and saw seven black swans gliding through the water like long-necked boats. Was that why Blossom wanted to be a swan? So that she could stay here always?

'Leave your case. We'll get it later,' Blossom said. And she led the way down the path.

It was a steep path and the bush crowded in on both sides. But there were wooden steps and a rail for the tricky bits. And there was something else as well.

The café was crouched at the bottom, gazing out to sea. It was a place, thought Miranda, where Blossom's bumper sticker just might be right. If magic did happen, then it very likely would happen right here.

At first the tin roof was all she could see, and that was a brilliant blue and covered all over with butterflies the size of dinner plates. Further down she saw windows peering from under the roof. And when at last she could see the whole building, she was utterly, totally rapt.

It was a long, low wooden cottage with a bit of a lean and a sag, and it wore its roof slightly crooked. But what did that matter when every wall, every door panel, every window-frame and shutter was painted in lolly colours, like a bag of jellybeans?

It sat in a kitchen garden that Miranda knew belonged to a world of long ago; a world that Theodelinda would have known. Fat peas and beans dangled on vines that clambered all over trellises. Beds of lettuce, rows of shallots, raspberry canes and a strawberry patch basked in the sunlight that sprinkled down between the leaves of the trees. Right in the middle was a herb garden set out in the shape of a wheel. The smell of mint and rosemary and thyme was mixed up with the smell of earth and sea. Miranda could have stayed there longer, just drifting around like one of the bumble bees. But 'This way!' Blossom told her, and Miranda followed her round to the front.

The café sat on solid ground, but its deep veranda hung

over the beach. As Miranda climbed up the wooden steps, she could make out some shadowy figures. The way they sprawled on the veranda floor, half propped against the wall, made her think they were customers who'd collapsed from thirst because the café was closed.

'Hi, guys!' sang out Blossom.

'Love the *wicked* hat!' someone cried. And it turned out that these were friends of Blossom, and her part-time staff.

Zeus and Zephyr were a couple who had hairdos exactly the same: dreadlocks sprouting out of their heads and threaded with coloured beads. Zeus also had a beard, and rings in his ear and top lip. Those and a ragged pair of shorts were the only things he wore. Zephyr's rings were through her nose and on each of her bare toes. She was wearing a sarong and a bra, and feeding a plump brown baby who wore nothing at all.

The baby was called Running Water, which seemed like the right name for him. There were a couple of damp patches on the floorboards to show where he'd been.

When introductions were made, Blossom told Miranda that Zeus was an utterly brilliant songwriter and Zephyr had the gift of second sight. So she could see that they'd both be pretty useful around the place.

Not counting Running Water, that made a staff of three. If they needed Miranda to help as well, the café was obviously flat out. No doubt they were resting up after one busy rush and waiting for the next.

Without exactly hurrying, everyone began to move. After a yawn and a stretch, Zeus set off to fetch Miranda's suitcase from the Kombi. Blossom pulled off her boots and wandered inside barefoot. Zephyr said she'd be in as soon as Running Water had burped.

'Come on,' Blossom called to Miranda. 'Come and see what I've done.'

So Miranda went inside and looked at the Cosmos Café, and the Cosmos Café looked back at her. It did this through one enormous red eye that was painted on the wall. The eye had more black liner around it even than Kelly's, and it stared the way Miranda's English teacher, Mrs Crumpstone, stared when she was giving a comprehension test. As if it thought you might be up to something even when you weren't.

And that wasn't all. There was a lot more really weird stuff all over the custard yellow walls.

Miranda blinked at a pink naked lady skipping through some flowers. That was OK, but why did she have a vine growing out of her belly button?

The black swans were there, a pair of them floating beak to beak, their necks so entwined that one false move would have meant instant strangulation.

A whopping fish had flipped out of the water. It had a dumb-struck look on its face, which could have been because it had frogs, snakes and lizards popping out of its mouth.

'We knocked the two front rooms into one, and I did all the painting myself.' Blossom whirled her arms at the artwork. 'It's the cosmos! All of creation!'

'I can see that,' said Miranda. She just hadn't seen it all in one place before.

The floor was green and crawling with giant bugs. Stars, meteors and planets whizzed around the ceiling. Mountains loomed, rivers rushed, trees twined, birds perched and beasts prowled, all in colours that made Miranda's head spin.

The tables were painted with the signs of the zodiac. Miranda sat down with a bump at Taurus the Bull. It had been a long morning, and she hoped very much that somebody would soon say something about lunch.

Sure enough, Zephyr's second sight kicked in and she got busy behind the counter. 'One orange, spinach and wheatgerm smoothie coming up!' she called. 'It's a meal in a glass and you'll love it!'

Here her psychic powers let her down. Miranda took one look at the foaming glass of greenish-brown gloop, and she did not love it. It made her think of chicken poo that had been put through a blender.

But Blossom must have had psychic powers too. She quickly took the glass and said, 'Yum, my favourite!' Then she asked Zephyr to make plain apple juice and a pitta bread roll with salad and goat's cheese for Miranda.

At least Miranda could eat that, but hot chips on the side would have made it a bit more filling.

All of a sudden Zeus zoomed through the door, minus the suitcase, but wild-eyed with excitement. 'Customers!' he yelled.

Zephyr scooped Running Water off the floor and dumped him in Miranda's lap. Then she ran to get a mop to fix up his latest puddle. Blossom raced behind the counter and scrambled into a big green pinafore. Zeus grabbed a guitar from somewhere, sat on a stool and started to strum the strings and drone down his nose, 'Oh, the pain, the pain, when you left me. The tears I cried when you went away.'

The middle-aged couple who walked in looked nervous. Miranda could understand that: the giant eye and the flowering belly button alone were enough to freak anybody out. But the woman clutched her husband's arm and they bravely picked their way through the giant bugs to the counter.

'Hello there! Glorious day! But we could do with rain. Unless you're on holiday. You don't want rain on your holiday!' Blossom blurted.

'Have a seat! Have a menu! Have anything you like!' Zephyr babbled as she wielded her mop.

'I think I'll just jump in the ocean and die!' Zeus sang.

The woman said that um, um, tea and cakes would be nice.

Blossom asked if they'd like peppermint, chamomile or dandelion tea. While they were thinking about that, she showed them some muffins in a glass case.

'But they're green!' the woman said.

Blossom agreed that they were. But that was because they were made of seaweed and oatbran. 'Enormously healthy,' she said.

The couple looked at each other, and then the man looked at his watch. 'It's a bit early for afternoon tea,' he decided. 'We might just leave it for now.' And the pair of them were out the door before you could say 'organic'.

Everybody sagged and sighed, and Zeus crashed a deep, dark chord on the guitar.

'We lost them!' wailed Blossom. 'Real live customers, and they got away!'

Miranda could see that this was a disaster for them, but she had one of her own. A warm, wet trickle was seeping through the knees of her jeans. Running Water had done it again.

Chapter 7

Miranda stood under the shower while it dripped cold water on her head one drop at a time. Tap twiddling made no difference. This was as good as it got.

She'd managed to collect enough water in the sponge to wash herself down, but now she had another problem. No way could she put her soggy jeans back on, and she still didn't have her suitcase.

In the end she put on her undies and blouse, wrapped a towel round her waist and went out into the passage that ran through the middle of the house from the café to the back door. There were rooms crammed down both sides of the passage. Hers was right next to the bathroom and had a smiley sunflower painted on the door.

It was only a small room, with just a bed, a dressing table, a wardrobe and a rug. But, like the bay, she'd loved it at first sight. The walls were the colour of sunshine and the window looked out into flowering banksia bushes and the path that led round the side of the house.

It felt good to be by herself for a while. She sat down on the bed and wondered how long she could stay there before she had to solve the problem of having nothing to wear on her bottom half.

She had a rash where her jeans had chafed, and her blouse felt tight under the arms. All at once she started to feel like what she was. A big fat lump. This happened quite often to Miranda, and it wrecked her happiest moments.

There was a tap at the door and Blossom asked, 'Can I come in?'

'OK.'

Blossom had Miranda's suitcase in one hand and a bundle of stuff in her other arm. 'Sorry,' she said. 'We ran out of water. We have to collect rainwater in a tank, and I keep forgetting to pump it up to the house.'

'OK.'

'Mim,' said Blossom. 'You can tell me to butt out if you want.' She dropped the bundle of stuff on the bed. 'But everything kind of hangs loose here, and I wondered if you'd like to try these.'

Miranda didn't tell her to butt out. She let Blossom show her how to tie the batik-patterned Balinese cloth around her waist so that it flowed to her ankles in soft red-and-gold folds. She changed her blouse for a big baggy yellow muslin shirt and put a floppy raffia hat on her head. And, just like that, she was loose and light and free, wiggling her bare toes on the floorboards, with absolutely nothing to weigh her down.

But something was weighing Blossom down. Her ex-half-sister-in-law suddenly flopped onto the bed and cried, 'Oh, Mim! Help! I think I've goofed big-time!'

Miranda sat down beside her and it all came pouring out.

When Magnus had dumped Blossom, first she felt really hurt, and then she got really mad. She wanted to show him that she didn't need him. So she'd travelled around looking for a new life, and she'd found it at Mariners Bay. The idea of the Cosmos Café had come all in a rush, and it had seemed such a good idea at the time.

'But nobody ever comes here!' Blossom wailed. 'It's so out of the way, hardly anybody finds it!' Then she did a totally un-Blossom thing and burst into tears. 'I'll be ruined! Bankrupt! You've got to help me, Mim!'

Miranda was totally confused. Of course she would help. But how could she? She didn't have any money. She didn't have anything.

'You've got imagination.' Blossom smiled hopefully through her tears. 'You have all those way-out things going on in your head. And that's what I need. A way-out idea to get people to come to the bay!'

Miranda couldn't remember anybody ever before telling her she had something they needed. Now she felt light enough to float up to the ceiling.

'I'll think of something,' she promised, and she gave Blossom a hug.

Then they went back to the veranda, where the rest of the staff were busy doing things like painting their toenails silver and watching the tide come in. Running Water was asleep in a beanbag, thankfully with a nappy on.

Zeus and Zephyr liked the new lighter-than-air Miranda.

'What does she have the spirit of?' Zephyr asked. And Miranda was happy enough to be able to laugh and say, 'A whale, maybe? A hot air balloon?'

Zephyr took her over to the veranda rail and pointed towards the horizon. 'See that hill?' she asked. 'See how curvy and comfortable it is? See how it lies there between the sea and the sky, all covered in forest and soft and green?'

Miranda looked, and she could see that the hill did look like a big cushiony person lying down.

'All kinds of creatures come to that hill,' Zephyr told her. 'It keeps them safe and happy, and it's really, really beautiful.' She smiled at Miranda. 'I think you've got the spirit of that hill.'

Miranda thought of Judy and hot chocolate and hugs. She thought of nests and burrows and warm, safe places, and she didn't mind having the spirit of a hill.

Then Zeus gave another huge stretch and said it must be nearly time to go home. Miranda wondered how they were going to do that. Apparently they lived on the other side of the soulless town, but there was no sign of anything but the Kombi parked nearby. Was Blossom going to drive them?

Blossom wasn't. A few minutes later they all wandered up to the road to wait for George.

George lived in the soulless town but spent most of his time out of it. Every day he drove his ute round and round the loop between the town, the village and the bay. He collected the mail, he delivered the mail. He picked up and delivered groceries, livestock, pretty much anything that anyone might want picked up or delivered. And he also ran a sort of taxi service. If his passengers didn't have cash, they paid him with whatever they did have. This afternoon Zephyr had a dozen seaweed muffins for him.

George arrived, wild-haired and toothless. Grinning gummily through the open window, in true Mariners Bay fashion he told Miranda who she was. Then he handed her a pale blue envelope with her name written on it. 'Found it under my wiper,' he said. 'Dunno who put it there.'

Miranda stared at the envelope while George's passengers climbed aboard and settled among the hay bales and craypots and crates of chooks. As they rattled off, she opened it.

The message, in beautiful curly writing on pale blue paper, was short. 'Once there were mermaids.' No name, nothing. What did it mean?

'Search me,' said Blossom when Miranda showed it to her. 'Life's full of strange messages.'

Miranda's life wasn't, not usually. But perhaps in Mariners Bay people wrote weird things on bits of paper and gave them to each other all the time.

'Why don't you go for a walk?' Blossom suggested. 'You might get an idea for the café.'

So Miranda put the envelope in her shirt pocket to wonder about later and set off along the grass verge.

Theodelinda walked alone along the edge of her kingdom by the sea. An ocean-scented breeze fluttered the silken hair under her hat and the sun kissed her golden skin. Graceful as a deer, she began to run, her bare feet skimming over the grass.

Nobody had mentioned blackberry briars. Youch! Miranda hopped on one foot, swayed, toppled, and slithered down the slope to land with a thump at the bottom.

She lay there for a while wondering how many bones she'd broken. Then she tried standing up. Everything seemed to be working all right, but now she had something else to worry about. The whole world had gone dark and a voice like a galah with bronchitis was screeching, 'That's right! Break yer flamin' neck, why don'tcha?'

She solved the first problem by pulling her hat up from over her eyes. Immediately she wished she hadn't, because the first thing she saw was an Aboriginal hunter without a stitch on, pointing a spear straight at her.

For a second she thought it might have been him who'd been yelling. Then she realised that it couldn't have been, because he was carved out of wood. She also realised that she'd tumbled into somebody's back yard. Some yards have garden gnomes, but this one had wooden carvings, everywhere.

What she had landed in was a Dreaming, with Aboriginal people and native animals and birds all mixed up with bunyips, yowies and other mysterious beasts. It was unreal, magical, and a whole heap better than garden gnomes.

But there was nothing unreal about the old man making his way down the steps of the wooden beach shack. His stubbled face was as crinkly as a screwed-up paper bag and he was actually shaking his fist.

'Idjut!' he yelled. He stomped through the Dreaming until he was close enough for Miranda to see dark eyes blazing at her from under grey, scrubby eyebrows. 'Did you hurt yerself?'

he asked. She shook her head, so he started yelling again. 'You rich bludgers! You think you can do whatever you want!'

Miranda had been called a lot of things in her life, but rich wasn't one of them. And she hadn't fallen over a cliff because she wanted to. But now didn't seem a good time to stop and argue.

'Nice to have met you,' she blurted. Then she turned and ran.

'You're going the wrong way!' he shouted after her. She didn't know why he thought so, but she didn't stop to discuss it. She just kept on running along the beach, round a little rocky headland and home to the Cosmos Café.

Chapter 8

'That would have been Jack Brannigan.' Blossom was in the kitchen chopping up vegetables for dinner. She'd been worried about Miranda's fall until she was sure no damage was done. But she quickly reassured her about the old man. 'He's a cranky old codger. But he's OK.'

Miranda wasn't so sure about that. But she did tell Blossom about the Dreaming.

'Fantastic, isn't it?' Blossom said. 'I've only seen it from the road. But Jack's Aboriginal himself, and I guess that's his way of saying so.'

Miranda didn't think that could be right. 'He doesn't look Aboriginal,' she said.

'What we look like isn't always what we are,' Blossom said. 'There are people who'll tell you there are no Aborigines left in Tasmania. But they're here all right. They're descended from Aboriginal women who had children by white settlers.'

Miranda had been told at school that the last Tasmanian

Aborigines had died about a hundred years ago. But now Blossom was telling her that there were still Tasmanians with Aboriginal blood, and proud of it, too.

'Back when Jack was a child, they had it really rough,' Blossom said. 'They weren't all white and they weren't all black, so they didn't fit in anywhere.'

Miranda knew what she meant. People who don't fit in get dumped on. She wished she'd stopped and talked longer with Jack, instead of running away.

Her face must have shown what she was thinking, because Blossom quickly said, 'I've heard Jack's story and it's not all bad. He had a wife named Mavis, and she was an absolute gem. They lived in the town and he had a carpenter's shop and was happy enough for years. But when Mavis died he went back to thinking that life was a real bummer. So he built that shack, and he fishes a bit, does his carving, and that's about it.'

Except for his Dreaming, Miranda thought.

The phone started to ring. It was for Miranda, and the babble on the other end was Brian and Judy saving on the call by both talking at once.

'Arrived all right then weather like there? Off tomorrow Blossom OK miss you HoHo New Guinea. Send a letter nice time darling forget to clean your teeth as soon as we get there love you!'

Miranda thought she got most of it, but then Kelly came on and things became clearer. She was over the moon about moving into Melanie's place, and did she have news for Miranda!

The Great Jacinta Jacques Yacht Cruise had gone completely pear-shaped, because Jacinta was the worst sailor ever. For a whole day and night she'd lain in her bunk spewing into a bucket. It was one way to spend a holiday, but Mr Jacques had got so fed up with her moaning that he'd turned the yacht round and brought her home.

Now Jacinta was staying with her totally boring aunt, Amy had been sent to her uncle's farm, and Mr and Mrs Jacques were sailing to the Barrier Reef without them.

Miranda was really happy that she'd ended up in Mariners Bay.

Blossom steamed the vegies with herbs and served them up in some kind of yoghurt sauce. And they tasted much better than steamed vegies are supposed to.

While they were eating dinner in the empty café, Miranda got her first really brilliant idea. It came when she heard a creepy shuffling and scuffling in the ceiling over her head.

'What's that?' she asked.

'It's a possum,' said Blossom.

'It could be a ghost,' said Miranda.

'No,' Blossom said. 'It's a possum.'

But Miranda wasn't going to give up on her idea just like that. 'Trust me,' she said to Blossom. 'That's a ghost you've got up there.'

When they'd finished the washing up they went into the living room. It was small and wonderfully untidy and stuffed with beanbags and old armchairs. There was no TV or DVD, just a very old record player and a bookcase so crowded with books that the overflow had piled up on the floor. But after they'd been sitting there for a while, Miranda began to see other things.

High up on top of the bookcase, not far from where the ghost walked, a pair of green eyes looked down at her from a tiny brown knobbly troll face.

Among the flowers in the fireplace a griffin was hatching out of its egg.

And instead of curtains, the windows were hung with shimmering dragonflies. Their bright wings were made from the wrappers of Hughey McDewey's Super Chewy Toffees.

Blossom saw her looking and laughed. 'Come with me,' she said. 'I'll show you where I do my thing.'

So Miranda followed her down the passage to a studio just inside the back door.

Blossom's thing was making beautiful objects out of goodness knows what. Wrapping paper, driftwood, bits of wire and coloured glass, seashells, beads and buttons, scraps of cloth and silken thread had been turned into dragons, unicorns, birds of paradise, angels and the huge butterflies that Miranda had seen on the roof.

This was Blossom's Dreaming and Blossom's magic. Miranda could have stayed there for ages, just looking, but then the phone started ringing again.

Blossom answered it. 'Hang on,' she said. Then she called out, 'Do we have a Celtic Warrior Princess? She's wanted on the phone!'

How embarrassing. Miranda got ready to tell Kelly 'Not funny', but a voice that wasn't Kelly's said, 'Hiya, Highness! It's the Mangler here. Do you want to come round tomorrow?'

Once she'd got over the shock, Miranda didn't think so.

'I'm going to be busy,' she said.

'No, you're not,' Nygel answered in his cleverdick way. 'Nobody's busy down there. You can borrow Sofie's bike if you want, and we'll go for a bit of a burn.'

Miranda said she'd have to ask. How did she get out of this?

A fat lot of help Blossom was. 'Not a problem!' she said. 'Zephyr'll be here by ten, and we need a few things from the shop. So I can run you over there, and George can bring you back.'

Terrific. Miranda had wanted to work on her plan tomorrow. Now she was stuck with Nygel the Nerd.

She slept that night with her strange message under her pillow and the sound of the sea rolling in on the beach.

Not surprisingly, she dreamed of mermaids.

Chapter 9

The next day was hot, really hot. Blossom found Miranda another big shirt and a pair of baggy drawstring pants.

She still didn't know why Nygel had asked her out. Probably so he could have a fight with her, but she didn't think she could be bothered with that. Her idea was looking better all the time and she wanted to get going with it.

When they arrived at the supermarket, Nygel was building a pyramid out of toilet rolls.

'Sofie!' he shouted. 'Royalty's arrived!' He made a deep bow and knocked the pyramid over with his rear end.

'Stumble-bum!' said Miranda, as toilet rolls took off in every direction. She and Blossom started to help him pick them up. Miranda wondered if he'd noticed her New Look. Probably not, because boys don't. She saw that he was wearing the same T-shirt as yesterday.

Sofie appeared, all smiles, and said she was so happy that Nygel and Miranda were friends.

Friends? Miranda wasn't sure about that. But she remembered Blossom saying that Nygel came to Mariners Bay when his mother was away. So the poor woman was probably back in the rest home or wherever.

'How's your mother?' she asked.

Nygel's emu eyes stared at her. 'She's fine,' he said. 'How's yours?'

But if Nygel didn't want to tell her much, Sofie certainly did.

'Look!' she cried, 'I will show you!' Dashing to the newsagency rack, she pulled out a glossy magazine and flicked through the pages to the middle. She stuck the magazine under Miranda's nose and stabbed at a photograph. 'See!'

Miranda read the headline: 'Glitter and Glitz at Vienna Opera House.' Then she looked at the photograph. What she saw was a tall, beaky-faced, dark-haired man in a dinner suit, and a slim blonde woman in a dark red cloak fastened with a jewelled brooch. The woman had a silver circlet around her crinkly hair, and she was smiling mysteriously into the camera.

'Best-selling Australian author Rhiannon Fayn arrives at the première with her archeologist husband Clive Featherstone.' Miranda read the caption twice and it said the same thing both times. She looked at Nygel. He had his hands deep in his pockets and his shoulders hunched. And, yes, thirty years older and with hair, he would have looked like Clive Featherstone.

'Rhiannon Fayn is your *mother*?' she asked him slowly.

'So?' said Nygel with a scowl, picking up a motorbike magazine.

'Such a beautiful lady!' said Sofie. 'And so famous!'

The scowl on Nygel's face grew blacker and Blossom suddenly became very interested in a pamphlet of recipes for lamb chops. Strange, considering she was a vegetarian. It was a tense moment, and it was about to get a whole lot tenser.

'Do you have any mail for Ambrazine?' asked a voice.

Miranda saw Blossom's face freeze and knew that she'd heard what she thought she'd heard.

A man with middle-aged movie star looks was standing at the post office counter. With him was a girl about Miranda's age, very dainty and slim. She had golden hair, eyes the colour of the sea, and a cute little sunfrock that showed a whole lot of silky, tanned skin with not a sunburn blister or a mozzie bite to be seen. They were beautiful people, and Ambrazines for sure. But what were they doing in a totally uncool place like Mariners Bay?

'Ambrazine?' asked Sofie, as though the man had said his name was Stinkydrawers. But then, Sofie was a good friend of Blossom's, so she would know all about Ambrazines.

Blossom was trying to hide behind the recipe pamphlet, but it wasn't big enough.

'Blossom!' the man cried in delight. 'It *is* Blossom, isn't it? You were married to Magnus!'

'Was I?'

The man was all crinkly-eyed smiles and flashing white teeth. 'Sure you were! I was at your wedding. Jerome Ambrazine, Celandine's cousin!'

Miranda gulped. If he was Celandine's cousin, then he'd probably been at her dad's first wedding too. But she didn't think she'd mention that right now.

'This is my daughter, Christabel,' said Jerome. Christabel's smile was much like his, except that hers had dimples in it.

Miranda had a sinking feeling. Just a moment ago she'd been in there with a good chance of being *the* friend of the son of Rhiannon Fayn. What chance now, with Little Miss Knock-Your-Socks-Off showing him her dimples?

Nygel glanced at Christabel, grunted, and went back to his motorbike magazine. It was rude of him, but it was the nicest thing he'd done since Miranda had met him.

Christabel's smile switched off like a torch. She looked straight through Miranda as if she didn't exist, and went off to look at shampoos and conditioners.

But Jerome wasn't through with charming the ladies yet. 'You're going to be seeing a lot of me,' he promised them. 'I've bought the Robinson place just round the headland. All very hush-hush just now, but what I'm going to do with it will be the best thing that's happened to this place.'

If Sofie really had been a goddess, the look she gave him would have made him about the right size to shove into one of her pigeonholes.

'There is no mail for Ambrazine,' she said.

'No?' Jerome seemed surprised. 'The stuff I'm expecting must have been emailed. I'll go and check.'

He turned again to Blossom and heaved a big sigh. 'Why would Magnus have left a gorgeous girl like you?' he asked.

'To do me a favour, I expect,' said Blossom, and Jerome laughed as though that was hilarious.

'See you again very soon,' he said. And he collected his daughter and left.

'Reptile!' hissed Sofie. 'Slithery snake!'

'He can't help it,' said Blossom. 'They're all like that.' She told them that she remembered Jerome all right. He'd left his fifth wife about a month before Magnus left Blossom.

Nygel came out of his magazine in the same dazed way that Miranda came out of one of his mother's books. 'That's the bike I'm going to have,' he told her.

Miranda looked, and said, 'Wow! Unreal!'

Something else pretty unreal dawned on her. Yesterday, cranky old Jack Brannigan had called her a rich bludger. And he'd yelled at her that she was running the wrong way home. Jack had thought she was Christabel Ambrazine. Not an easy mistake to make!

When Blossom had gone and Sofie was busy counting her postage stamps, Nygel took Miranda to the library. It was in the living room behind the plastic curtain, and it didn't have as many books as Blossom had at home.

There was a big sign that said NO EATING OR DRINKING, so Nygel got them a packet of chips and a fizzy drink each. But they didn't go near the books, they just sat at the table and talked, mostly about themselves.

Miranda told Nygel that she'd give anything to have hair like his mother's. He told her exactly what she'd have to give. 'Ninety-seven dollars, plus a tip, Rizzi Hair and Beauty, Melbourne.'

Nygel told Miranda he'd give anything to have a family like hers. It was no big deal having Rhiannon Fayn for a mother. Her real name was Brenda Featherstone, but not even her husband was allowed to call her that. The kids at boarding school all thought Nygel was really stuck up because he had a famous mother and never invited them to his place to meet her.

'Fat lot of good that'd do them,' he said. 'She's hardly ever there. Her and Dad are always travelling. And if she is home, she's writing and won't talk to anybody. If I want to know what she's up to I have to look on the Internet, same as any-body else.'

What Nygel didn't actually say, but Miranda guessed, was that Sofie was more like a mum to him. She was a widow with no children of her own, and the Featherstones had hired her to be Nygel's nanny from the day he was born until he was old enough to go to boarding school. Then they'd dumped her.

Just like Blossom, Sofie had found a new life in Mariners Bay. But Nygel's parents had got busier and busier, digging up history and writing stories about it. So they'd dug up good old Sofie, too, just so they could send Nygel to her in the school holidays.

Hearing that was enough to set Miranda off about the Ambrazines again. Then, somehow or other, she got onto Jacinta and Amy and the way she'd been shoved out by the yacht cruise that went down the gurgler.

'Good job you were,' said Nygel. 'Or you wouldn't be here.'

What was that supposed to mean? Was old Emu Features telling her he was glad she was here? Miranda tried to think of something nice, but not too wussy, to say back. Then she decided to do something else instead, and she showed him her secret message.

'What do you think it means?' she asked.

'Pretty obvious,' said Nygel. 'One of our many local nutters is into mermaids. They probably heard that you're a fairy princess and thought you might be interested.'

Miranda sighed. Too bad the note didn't say 'Once there were hatchet murderers.' Then he might have taken more notice.

All the same, she decided to risk telling him her idea for getting visitors to the Cosmos. 'A ghost,' she said. 'Tourists love haunted places. If we spread it around that the café's got a ghost, lots of people will come.'

She waited for him to tell her it was a dumb idea, but he didn't.

'The *Bugle*,' he said. 'That's where we start.' He handed her the local paper and pointed to the phone. 'Go for it!'

Miranda dialled the number printed at the top of the front page.

'The *Southern Boogle*,' cooed a woman's voice on the crackly line. 'How can I help yoo?'

Miranda got straight to the point. 'We've got a ghost in our roof,' she said.

There was silence, except for the crackling. Then the voice asked, 'Har you sure you don't want the Har SPC Hay?'

'No,' said Miranda. 'I want a reporter to come to the Cosmos Café and write a story about this ghost.'

'How long has it been there?' the voice wanted to know.

'Who knows? Years and years!'

Still sounding doubtful, the woman said she would have a word with their Mr Bloom. He might come this afternoon if he could fit them in.

After she'd hung up, Miranda had a thought. 'What if the ghost only walks at night? Most of them do, don't they?'

Nygel didn't think that was a problem. Mr Bloom would have to sleep over. If he was going to write a really good story, he'd need to spend the night in the haunted house.

He was right, of course. But Miranda thought they ought to cycle over to the Cosmos after lunch and let Blossom know that Mr Bloom was coming. Especially if he was going to stay the night.

Chapter 10

Surprise, surprise, when they got back to the Cosmos it was empty except for Zephyr and Blossom. They were making vegetarian pizzas that would end up in the freezer along with all the other uneaten stuff. But all that was about to change, and Miranda explained how.

'I see,' said Blossom. 'You've invited the media to meet our possum.'

Zephyr was a lot more positive. She said she often sensed Strange Presences hovering in the Cosmos.

Blossom said she wished the Strange Presences would order something from the menu instead of just hanging about.

Nygel had his bathers in his backpack and he went to the bathroom to change. Miranda was dying for a swim, but she was worried about what she looked like in her bathers. Then she saw what Nygel looked like in his and stopped worrying.

Miranda was a good swimmer. Jacinta Jacques said it was

because she had so much blubber to keep her afloat. But Nygel had a thrash-and-splash style that didn't really take him anywhere, so Miranda thrashed and splashed as well, just so that he wouldn't think she was showing off.

After that they got into hats, shirts and sunscreen and just lay on the beach. The swans glided by and it was all very sunny and peaceful.

Miranda gazed out across the bay. *Once there were mermaids.* Mermaids swimming in these bright-as-glass waters? Mermaids basking on these sea-smoothed rocks? She could see them inside her head in the same way as she saw Theodelinda. But the mermaids were different. They were in someone else's head too. And that someone had sent her a note.

'Here he is!' Nygel jumped up and shook his sandy towel all over her. 'The man we've all been waiting for – Bloom from the *Boogle*!'

Miranda squinted up at the car park and saw someone getting out of a green beetle car.

'It's either him or a customer!' she cried. And they raced up the beach to find out.

By the time their visitor had reached the bottom of the slope, Nygel, Miranda, Blossom and Zephyr were all there to meet him.

'Angus Bloom from the *Bugle*,' he said. He sounded a bit

nervous, but they could see he was dead serious about being a newsman. He had serious grey eyes behind horn-rimmed glasses, a serious white shirt with a navy blue tie, and very seriously pressed trousers.

'I've come about the goat in your roof,' he informed them.

Blossom said, '*What?*', and the way she gaped made her seem a bit dumb.

Miranda remembered all that crackling on the phone line and quickly explained, 'It's not a goat, it's a ghost.'

Then it was Mr Bloom's turn to say, '*What?*' So Miranda told him about the scrabbling and scampering in the roof at night.

Mr Bloom ran his fingers through his hair, which was a bit long and floppy for someone so serious. 'I don't know,' he said. 'We don't do ghosts as a rule. We're mostly into sixtieth wedding anniversaries and babies born in cars. That sort of stuff.'

Blossom got a grip on herself and told Mr Bloom that she couldn't help him there. She'd barely made it to her second wedding anniversary, and she'd never had a baby, in a car or anywhere else.

Zephyr said she had a friend who'd had a baby in a tent. But that was five years ago, so it wasn't exactly news.

It was Nygel who got things back on track by telling Mr

Bloom that he should come back tonight and be prepared to sleep over.

'Just dinner, I think,' said Blossom firmly. 'The ghost usually walks while we're having dinner.' She asked Mr Bloom if he could come back at seven and he was pretty sure that he could. Then he said that he'd always meant to visit the Cosmos anyway, and could he order afternoon tea?

Miranda thought that Blossom was going to kiss him, but he got one of her brilliant smiles instead. 'Yes!' she cried. 'Come on in!'

Miranda was all set to follow, just to make sure that Blossom didn't blow it by offering him a seaweed muffin. But Zephyr said very quickly, 'Mim, Nygel, come and help me pick raspberries for tonight.'

Whatever it was that Mr Bloom ordered, he was a very slow eater. It was after five when he left, and by that time Zephyr had rattled off with George. Blossom said that Mr Bloom had listened very solemnly while she explained what the eye and the belly button and everything else meant. 'I think he might have the spirit of an owl,' she said.

Only Miranda heard Nygel mutter, 'Yeah, a stuffed one.'

All the same, Nygel was keen to be there when the ghost walked, so Blossom invited him to dinner too.

Mr Bloom was back by ten to seven. He'd changed into

another serious shirt and he was carrying a bunch of pink carnations. Miranda thought that maybe carnations were an antidote to ghosts, like garlic for vampires. But Mr Bloom gave the flowers to Blossom and asked her to call him Angus.

For someone who didn't have a lot of faith in the ghost idea, Blossom certainly did her best. She dropped the blinds to make the light all murky and lit two big candles at the Taurus table. It was a fabulously creepy way to eat vegetarian pizza, with or without a ghost.

Angus asked if they thought someone had actually died in their roof. Miranda said it could have been someone imprisoned up there for some ghastly crime, a murder perhaps? Then again it could have been the murder victim. Nygel asked Blossom if she'd painted over any bloodstains when she did the ceiling, but she said she couldn't remember.

At last the moment they were all waiting for arrived.

Scratch, scrabble, scamper, scamper. Everyone gazed up at the ceiling and listened.

'That's a possum,' said Angus Bloom. 'I've got one in my roof at home.'

Nobody spoke. But just for a moment there was a glimmer of something behind Angus's glasses that wasn't all that serious.

Then, 'Right!' said Blossom brightly. 'Who's for raspberries and cream?'

Chapter 11

How embarrassing. Every time Miranda thought about the
ghostly possum she felt like a total nerd.

How embarrassing. Every time Miranda thought about the
ghostly possum she felt like a total nerd.

Nygel kept telling her not to worry. Angus had enjoyed
himself in his own geeky way, and he had actually paid money
for his afternoon tea.

'All we need is a better idea,' Nygel said.

What did he mean, 'we'? It was Miranda's imagination that
was supposed to be doing the work. But right now her imagination seemed to be on vacation.

It was the next day, the very last day of the year, and she and
Nygel were sitting on the veranda steps throwing leftover pizza
crust to the seagulls. Not that there was much left to throw.
When Blossom had found out that Angus lived alone, she'd
made him up a huge doggy bag to take home.

They were also keeping an eye on Running Water, who was
crawling around under the veranda and eating sand. It didn't

72

seem to be doing him any harm and Nygel said it was probably another natural food, like seaweed.

Just to keep his brain active, Nygel was using it to count the number of hire coaches that went by without stopping at the Cosmos. He'd got up to five, which was four more than usual. Stretching his brainpower even further, he came to the conclusion that they could be on their way to some big bash at the Ambrazines' new place.

'That'd be right,' Miranda agreed.

Zephyr and Zeus were with Blossom in the kitchen. For once they weren't cooking for the café, but for the New Year's Eve beach party that Blossom was giving that night.

Somebody close by had started a party already, and a wild one at that. Music blared, voices screeched and sang and yahooed, and it all seemed to be arriving up in the car park.

Nygel jumped to his feet and the seagulls scattered. 'Yee-hah!' he yelled. 'It's the Barneys on their bus!'

'Who?' Miranda fished out Running Water from under the veranda and held him close, waiting for the rowdy hoons to descend on them.

'St Barnabas's Church!' Nygel couldn't have looked happier if it had been his street gang that had arrived. 'They're kind of weird, but kind of cool. The Bishop closed their building down last year because they were so small. But they bought this old bus and they just keep on having Church Outings!'

The screen door crashed open and Blossom dashed out with Zephyr close behind, both of them off the planet with excitement.

'I don't *believe* it!' Blossom shrieked. 'A Barneys' Outing, *here*! Quick, Zeph, what've we got?'

Zephyr gabbled off the menu, including what they'd cooked for the party. 'Masses!' Blossom cried. 'We can do it!'

Miranda, still clutching Running Water, just stood and watched as St Barnabas's Church came pouring down the steps.

First off the bus was the dead dog, very lively and wagging its tail. Then came the Terror of the Shopping Trolley, Mrs Lovelace. And behind her marched a whole bunch of people waving their arms and singing 'Onward, Christian Soldiers' at the top of their voices.

These were what were known around the place as Barneys. They came in all shapes and sizes, from a very little girl toting a bucket and spade to an incredibly ancient man who had to be carried down on a kitchen chair. As well as singing, this one was loudly beating a pair of bongos he had balanced on his lap.

'Rejoice! Rejoice!' the Barneys cried as they trooped round to the front of the café.

'We are! We are!' Blossom assured them. 'Come on in!'

Everyone was sure that someone else had rung and booked,

and Blossom was just as sure that they hadn't. But so what? It was a fabulous Church Outing anyway.

The Barneys took one look at the Cosmos and went right off the planet.

'Oh, rejoice!' said Mrs Lovelace, all shiny-eyed. 'It's the whole world! The whole of creation!'

Then they launched into a really upbeat version of 'He's Got the Whole World in His Hands', with Zeus on guitar and the ancient Barney on bongos.

After that Mrs Lovelace did her liturgical dance. Barefoot, and with floating scarves tied around her hair, her wrists and her waist, she skipped and dipped and skittered and swayed and only wobbled a little bit when she was poised on one leg.

Then there was a time of prayer. Mrs Lovelace said they could ask for anything they liked, as long as it was good. So, very quietly, Miranda asked for a super brilliant idea to save the café.

After some more loud singing, it was time for lunch. The Barneys were as enthusiastic about eating as they were about everything else. Thank goodness there'd been extra cooking today.

Miranda was in the kitchen buttering yet another batch of herbed scones when somebody else came in. She thought it must be Blossom or Zephyr, but it was Mrs Lovelace. The old lady smiled with her brilliant blue eyes, then spoke in her soft, burring voice. 'You know, there used to be mermaids here, my dear.'

Miranda stared, and Mrs Lovelace smiled again. 'I knew the moment I saw you that you'd believe it,' she said.

'Tell me,' said Miranda. So Mrs Lovelace did.

'Oh, yes, they were here sure enough. Right here in Mariners Bay. Only the name got changed because folks stopped remembering things right. At the beginning it wasn't Mariners Bay, it was Marina's Bay – a pretty name, not unlike your own, dear.

'And who was Marina? Well, only the loveliest mermaid any sailor could hope to meet, even in his dreams. But here's the sad thing. Although she had glorious golden hair and eyes as green as her tail, the one man Marina fell in love with had no feelings at all for her. She could have been a cod fillet on the fishmonger's slab for all Captain Hornpipe cared.

'This was in Devon, England, in eighteen seventy-three. And Devon is where my family's from, so that's how I know it's all true. He was a handsome rogue, this Captain Hornpipe, but his only love was the sea. And the day he set sail for Tasmania, all the girls stood and wept on the shore. But once a mermaid has given her heart, it's given for evermore. So Marina just started swimming, and she followed his ship all the way.

'And that's not all. By windsong and wavesong and whale-song, all across the seven seas, the story was told of Marina and what she was doing for love. And mermaids from every part of the world came just to be in the swim, splashing and singing and twirling their tails all around Captain Hornpipe's ship.

'Then, when the voyage was almost over, up blew a mighty storm. Captain Hornpipe and his crew tried to shelter right here in this bay. But their ship got smashed up on the rocks and every last one of them drowned.'

'Oh!' Miranda could see and hear it all. And she didn't want to think of such a terrible thing happening in her beautiful, peaceful bay.

But Mrs Lovelace was still smiling. 'Leastways,' she said, 'some said they drowned. But others believed, and I believe too, that they were carried in mermaid arms to live in a paradise under the sea with their beautiful mermaid wives.'

Miranda couldn't see why not. It was a whole heap better than drowning, and a lot more romantic too.

'And people actually saw mermaids here?' she asked.

'Absolutely, dear,' Mrs Lovelace said. 'My grandmother saw them when she was about the same age as you. But that, of course, was a long time ago. Nobody sees them now.'

No, well, they wouldn't, would they? Nobody seemed to see anything like that any more. Miranda wondered why.

Without being asked, Mrs Lovelace answered that question. 'Nobody cares,' she said. 'Nobody believes. They don't as much as think about mermaids, so why should they see them?'

On the other side of the bead curtain, the Barneys started rejoicing again. That reminded Miranda that they were waiting for more scones, so she picked up the tray.

'I just had to tell you, dear,' Mrs Lovelace said. 'I thought you would want to know.'

Chapter 12

In a world where people can no longer see mermaids, in the space of an hour Miranda got an email from Papua New Guinea (via the post office) and a phone call from Sydney. Brian and Judy sent her a page of hugs and kisses. Kelly had broken up with Bronson, but was going to the *biggest ever* New Year's Eve rage with this *gorgeous* hunk who sang in a rock band. Brian couldn't say anything about that, could he?

For a teary hour Miranda really, really missed them. But later on, sitting on a rug between Nygel and Blossom and watching sparks from the driftwood bonfire shooting into the darkness, she was so glad that she was right here with these people, right here in this place.

She looked at the faces in the firelight. Blossom was glowing like a bonfire herself, still rapt about the Barneys' Outing. Nygel, who was turning from a skinhead into a stubblehead, had all kinds of grotesque expressions flitting across his face. It was like somebody zapping through the TV channels, with a horror movie on every one. But Miranda knew he was only practising different Mangler scowls inside his head and didn't know they were showing up on his face.

Goddesses are always at their best around leaping flames, and Sofie looked truly awesome as she piled lumps of baklava on picnic plates. They'd had cheese and spinach pasties, hommus dip, olive bread and sundried tomatoes. Now it was time for some deliciously sweet and gooey afters.

On the other side of the fire were Zeus and Zephyr, with Running Water asleep in a basket, and, surprise, surprise, Angus Bloom. Now, who could have invited him? Angus's idea of casual gear was a kind of cowboy outfit – plaid shirt, jeans and boots. But at least he was giving it a go.

Maybe it was all the sugar in Sofie's sweets. Maybe it was just because it was New Year's Eve and they were on a lonely beach on a little island somewhere between Australia and the Antarctic. Whatever it was, they started to sing silly songs and tell silly stories and laugh their socks off. Even Angus, who was the only one actually wearing socks. Miranda got so carried away that she risked a Hughey McDewey Super Chewy Toffee out of Nygel's Deluxe Christmas pack. And her braces survived it.

It was Blossom who first saw the shadowy figure hovering just beyond the firelight.

'Hey, Jack!' she called. 'Come and join the party!'

The only answer was a grunt, and the figure faded into the darkness. But a few minutes later Miranda noticed a rock that might not have been all rock. The humped-up lump on top could have been somebody sitting on it.

When it was almost midnight, and they'd run out of silliness and were just humming along to Zeus's guitar, Miranda told the story of the mermaids of Marina's Bay. She told it in her clearest and best storytelling voice, with all the feeling that was inside her. And while she was telling it, she began to be filled with something that was more of a dream than an idea.

What was it that Mrs Lovelace had said? Nobody believed any more. Nobody as much as thought about mermaids any more. So why should they see them?

But what if people did believe? What if they did think about them? What if there was so much believing in Marina's Bay that the mermaids came back?

'Angus,' she said, when she'd finished telling the story, 'would you write about that in the *Bugle*?'

She knew he'd think about it seriously, and he did. 'I could do some research,' he said. 'Find out if there was a wreck in the bay at that time.'

'Yes!' Blossom gave him one of her smiles and Miranda knew it was going to be a cinch.

'The paper's having a two-week break,' Angus said. 'But I could probably do something after that.'

Then they were all very quiet, just gazing into the fire and thinking about mermaids.

From somewhere just round the headland a whining screech suddenly ripped across the sky. Then another and another. The night was filled with explosions like rifle fire. Fountains of green, red and silver stars showered through clouds of coloured smoke. It was loud and it was bright and it went on and on. Jerome Ambrazine and his coachloads of guests were celebrating the New Year with a whopping great firework display.

Running Water began to shriek almost as loudly as the rockets. The figure on the rock leaped up with waving fists. 'Rich bludgers! Think you can do what you like!'

The magical midnight moment was shattered and now it was the Ambrazine Show.

Nygel, mouth open and emu eyes popping, kept squeaking, 'Wow! Awesome! Unreal!' But he was the only one who thought so.

Miranda scrunched herself up and stuck her fingers in her ears. Over and over she told herself that she still had her dream, and no Ambrazine was going to wreck that.

The next morning everything seemed to be on her side. The weather was softly warm, calm and still, with the bay shining in all its colours and not a sound but the swish of small waves on the sand.

George dropped off Zephyr, and Nygel turned up on his bike. So with those two and Blossom, Miranda had enough to get started on her dream.

When she explained it, Blossom and Zephyr caught on straight away. Nygel took a bit longer.

'So, you reckon if we think hard enough about mermaids, we can make them appear?' he asked.

'Sort of,' said Miranda. 'It's like, if we don't believe in something, then it has a hard time being real. But if we do believe, really believe, then maybe it can.'

Nygel thought about that. 'Like the power of positive thinking,' he said. Then, somewhere inside his bony, stubbly skull, a light went on. 'Hey! We could think up werewolves and zombies and all those dead guys from under the sea!' he suggested.

Miranda started to tell him to go home to his motorbike magazines. But Blossom put her arm around him and said, 'Why not go for mermaids first? If it works, you can go on to bigger things.'

As usual, nothing else was happening at the Cosmos, so they went down to the beach to start dreaming up mermaids. Blossom and Zephyr sat cross-legged, eyes closed and faces under their raffia hats as calm as the sea. Nygel sprawled face down on a towel, probably trying for zombies despite what Blossom had said. Miranda just gazed out to sea, where even the swans were like floating statues. Beyond them, and just as still, Jack Brannigan sat with a fishing line over the end of his boat.

When Miranda had turned six, Judy made her a fairy frock for her birthday. It was pink satin and net, with a pair of gauze wings that fastened to her shoulders with elastic. And when Miranda had those wings on, it seemed very, very possible that she could fly.

She used to crouch on the back veranda and look down at the ground below. The difference between being able to fly and not being able to was as flimsy as the gauze of her wings. She could *feel* the lightness in her body, *feel* herself jumping off the veranda and not falling, but flying.

She never did fly, but for a long time she believed that she could. And that was the feeling she had now. Marina and all the other mermaids were so real that every part of her could feel their reality.

With a snarling, whining roar that left last night's fireworks for dead, something blasted out into the bay at about 10,000 kilometres an hour.

In a frantic flurry of wings the swans rose up from the water and headed for the horizon. Nygel got tangled in his own arms and legs as he tried to leap up. And the huge wash from whatever it was tipped Jack Brannigan out of his boat.

As Jack hit the water, Miranda's feet hit the sand. She pelted down the beach, but just before she reached the ocean she saw the old man, alive and afloat, hauling himself back on board.

Only then did she stop and look to see what it was that had shattered the peace and the mermaid dream. It looked like a giant transparent torpedo, and as it zoomed in an arc and headed back towards the point, she could see at least two people inside it.

Nygel couldn't have been more starry-eyed if a whole pack of Hell's Angels had suddenly learned to ride on water. But Blossom and Zephyr just sat there, totally stunned.

'The swans have gone,' said Miranda. And something choky and scared inside her wondered if all hope of mermaids had gone with them.

Chapter 13

It didn't take long for word to get around, especially when the torpedo thing started hooning around the bay two or three times a day. Everybody in town was pretty upset about that, except for one. And Sofie and Miranda fixed him. They sat Nygel down and explained, in short, simple words, that loud and fast didn't always mean good. In the end he seemed to catch on.

It was Sofie who had the first clues about what was happening. Mail started arriving at the post office for Jerome Ambrazine, Managing Director, Thrillboats Inc.

'Thrillboats!' she hissed at Blossom, Miranda and a wrinkled little man with the spirit of a tortoise who had come in to pick up their own mail. 'I will give him thrills! I will rip off him everything but his socks. I will tie him by his ankles to the back of his boat and shoot him off to the Antarctic with his bare bum showing for all the world to see. Maybe that will be thrilling enough for him!'

It was an interesting idea, but Miranda didn't think Jerome
would be in it.

'Bags I drive the boat!' said Blossom.

The wrinkled man gave the whole matter some very serious
thought. Then he blinked his tortoise eyelids and said, 'What
we'll have to do is call a public meeting.'

So that's what they did. They called it for Friday night at the
Cosmos Café, because that was the only place big enough to
hold the public.

Nygel said he'd make posters to advertise the meeting. After
four hours on the computer he came up with the time, the
place and

WHADDA WE WANT? WHADDA WE SAY?

RACK OFF THRILLBOATS FROM OUR BAY!

'Oh, yes, absolutely brilliant!' sighed Miranda.

'It's cool,' he said. 'Writing runs in our family.'

But so much creative effort had burned him out, so Miranda
was the one who had to stick up the posters.

She put one in the supermarket window and went outside to
see what it looked like. And who should be standing reading it
but Christabel Ambrazine.

Just for a second their eyes met. Then a totally blank look
came over Christabel's face and off she went. Miranda didn't
care that Christabel had cut her dead. She didn't even notice

that Christabel's bottom looked fantastic in shorts. Well, she hardly noticed.

That night Blossom got a phone call from Jerome. He was delighted, *delighted* about the meeting. And he *welcomed* the opportunity to tell the wonderful people of Mariners Bay just how much good fortune was coming their way.

'Listen, pal,' Blossom told him. 'You know, and I know, that any fortune to be had will be going your way and nobody else's! So don't think you can con the people round here, because you can't!'

But off the phone she didn't sound nearly so sure. And her hair was completely on end, which was a bad sign.

'People *will* come to the meeting, won't they, Mim?' she asked.

And they did come. The Barneys were first. They had the dead dog with them, and were carrying the ancient one on his chair. He was bristling for a fight, but had his bongos with him in case it turned into a party.

George arrived with a uteload that included Zephyr and Zeus, even though they didn't live in Mariners Bay. Another out-of-towner was Angus.

After that the door just kept opening and people kept coming in. Sofie, all glittering eyes and crimson lipstick and fingernails, was in dragon lady mode tonight. And Nygel had come along in a black wetsuit that made him look like a stick of liquorice – especially as he had one of Sofie's black stockings over his head.

'What's with the weirdo outfit?' Miranda whispered as she slid into an empty seat behind him.

His answer was a bit muffled by the stocking, but it sounded like, 'SAS! Commando tactics! We'll sabotage his Thrillboats!'

Miranda wasn't sure if that was the way to go. But before she could say so, Jerome Ambrazine made his entrance. He made it smiling and waving like the President of the United States, all the way up to the table at the front where the tortoise man who had called the meeting was set up as chairman. Close behind Jerome came an incredibly good-looking, incredibly suntanned young man with gelled blonde hair and dazzling teeth. He smiled too, but he couldn't wave because he was using both hands to carry four huge leather cases.

Everybody knew the puddingy, wispy-haired figure puffing along behind. It was Councillor Quamby from the town without a soul. But they'd never before seen him carrying a giant cardboard cut-out of a Thrillboat full of cartoon people going crazy with excitement.

Last of all came Christabel, a real cutie-pie in her lolly pink pantsuit, but looking bored as usual.

Nobody was sure whether all this was supposed to be

happening or not. The chairman just sat and blinked. Councillor Quamby leaned the cut-out against the table and flopped into a chair in the front row. For a moment there was a flicker of expression on Christabel's face, and that was because she'd caught sight of Nygel. Her eyes widened and the corners of her mouth twitched. Then everything went deadpan again and she sat down next to the councillor.

If it was the chairman who was supposed to open the meeting, nobody had told Jerome. Flinging out his arms as though he wanted to hug the whole room, he cried, 'My dear, dear friends!' Like his daughter, he had a gobsmacked moment when he noticed that one of his dear friends was dressed as a tadpole, but he carried on regardless.

'Tonight is a very special night for all of us. Indeed, it is the beginning of a great and glorious future right here in Mariners Bay.' His eyes moved warmly and kindly along the rows, but skipped Nygel for obvious reasons. 'It will be a future marked by prosperity, progress and opportunity for you all . . .'

'That's a load of horse manure, and you know it!'

Nobody had noticed Jack Brannigan come in. But Jerome's smile was suddenly bouncing off the backs of heads as everybody turned round to look at the old man standing just inside the door. Pointing a quivering finger at Jerome, he proclaimed, 'You rich bludgers are all the same. All mouth and money!

But you never did nobody any good excepting for yerselves! A good kick up the backside's what you need!'

Jerome's eyes grew warmer and his smile grew cheesier. 'Thank you, sir. Your valuable comments are much appreciated. But if I can just have everyone's attention for now, there will be time for some general discussion at the end of the meeting.'

'Bull!' Jack growled.

But Jerome was already moving on. 'Later this evening we will be hearing from a man you all know and trust, your very own Councillor Fred Quamby.' He waited for applause but none came, so he moved on again. 'I know, I know, you're all wondering who is the handsome guy who's been so busy setting up our PowerPoint display!'

Judging by their nods of agreement, quite a few of the women present certainly were wondering.

The bronze hunk had unfurled a screen, set up a DVD player, and even managed to look good crawling under the table to find somewhere to plug in his cables. He was introduced as Jason Johnston Junior from the USA.

'Jason is my partner, and the designer of the Thrillboat,' Jerome told them. 'And the Thrillboat is *the* latest, *the* greatest, *the* most exciting concept in adventure holidays. It is the fastest, the most mind-blowing, positively sensational way to explore the wonderful world of water without getting wet.'

Miranda heard again the scream of high-speed engines hurtling across the bay. She saw the frightened flapping of swans' wings and felt the fading of her mermaid dream.

There was worse to come. Jason Johnston Junior started showing architectural drawings of the Robinson property. Only now it was called Oceana Park – 'Home of Thrillboats and All the Discerning Holidaymaker Dreams Of'.

'Ten luxury suites, each with its own jacuzzi,' crowed Jerome. 'The Seabreeze Restaurant, the Blue Wave Disco and the Silver Shores Bistro.'

Miranda looked along the row and saw the expression on Blossom's face. What hope had the Cosmos Café got against that lot? She wished she was close enough to give Blossom's hand a squeeze, and then she saw that Angus was doing just that.

And still Jerome raved on.

Theodelinda felt a tremor of indignation ripple through her slender body. Never before had her beloved people faced such an evil threat. This oily-tongued stranger was plotting to take away everything they held most dear. He took them for poor, ignorant peasants, helpless, leaderless and no match for his greedy plans. The tremor inside her turned to a blazing flame and she leaped to her feet. Clarion clear, her bell-like voice rang out. 'You shall not have your way! We shall fight you to the bitter end!'

'You tell him, girl!' Jack Brannigan yelled in a voice cracked with excitement.

Only then did Miranda realise that *she* had stood up and *she* had called out. She felt her cheeks begin to burn and her legs go wobbly.

Then Sofie jumped up too. Eyes flashing and crimson-nailed hands waving, she launched into a speech filled with such fire and passion that everyone, even Jerome Ambrazine, listened open-mouthed.

Unfortunately the speech was in Greek, but they all got the general idea of it.

'Yeah!' shouted somebody from the middle row. 'We'll fight you, mate! You know what you can do with yer Thrillboats, don'tcha!'

'Rejoice!' cried a voice that had to belong to a Barney. 'Fight the good fight! We shall overcome!'

Nygel stood on his seat and punched the air, uttering wild threats through his stocking.

The dead dog trotted up to the front and sniffed the cut-out Thrillboat. Then, to tumultuous cheers, it cocked its leg on it. The ancient Barney, thinking the party had begun, started beating his bongos.

Jason Johnston Junior's tan turned dark red, and he crawled back under the table. But Jerome stayed calm, a cold, hard calm that didn't have any kind of a smile in it. He waved his hands for quiet.

'I see,' he said. 'But let me warn you that this unfortunate, might I even say ungrateful, attitude will get you nowhere. The property has been purchased, a company has been registered and council approval has been granted. Testing of the Thrillboat will continue and Oceana Park will open. Nothing you can do will stop it.'

He shoved the soggy cut-out at Councillor Quamby and made an exit that wasn't as grand as his entrance, but not bad. Christabel, close behind him, had the door slammed in her face, but didn't as much as blink. Jack opened it for her and she sailed through as though she were Lady Alyce and he the lowest of her serfs.

That just left Jason Johnston Junior to pack up the display, but nobody took any notice of him. There was a huge buzzing and burbling all over the room until the chairman remembered that he was supposed to be in charge.

'Order! Order!' he called, and surprisingly he got it. Blinking ten times faster than usual, he asked, 'What are we going to do then?'

Nygel started mumbling loudly through his stocking about frogmen with pickaxes, but nobody seemed keen on that idea. It was Zeus who came up with a better one.

'A protest!' he cried. 'A demo! We'll sit on his ramp so he can't launch his Thrillboat!'

Zephyr and Sofie both shrieked, 'Yes!' and Blossom suddenly had her sparkle back.

Of course! A good old placard-waving, slogan-chanting protest. They hadn't had one of those in months.

Chapter 14

The Big Thrillboat Protest was fixed for the following Friday, and this time Miranda made sure she did the publicity herself. She designed posters with words like 'Beauty', 'Tranquillity' and 'Heritage', and Blossom decorated them by hand with pictures that matched the words.

They gave Nygel the job of making placards. He put a lot of effort, and paint, into them. But his wording was more along the lines of 'Bog off!', 'Blitz', 'Blast', and 'Blow 'em out of the water!'

The *Bugle* was still on holiday, and Angus said that if it was announced that Mariners Bay was to be the venue of the next Olympic Games, the local paper wouldn't open up to run the story. But he did send a poster and a press release to the *Hobart Mercury*. He also got Blossom an interview on Bottom End FM, the radio station that broadcast from a studio behind the chip shop in the town without a soul. The interview was at a quarter past five in the morning, but Blossom did a brilliant job of explaining to whoever was listening why Mariners Bay didn't need Thrillboats.

The next day, as a special news item, Bottom End announced that it had a new major sponsor, Mr Jerome Ambrazine. And Mr Ambrazine was offering a cash prize of $10,000 to the person who wrote the catchiest Thrillboats theme song.

Two days after that, the *Mercury* ran a double-page feature on the up-and-coming Oceana Park, with big cheesy photos of Jerome and Jason all over it.

That was the day the weather turned cold and wet, which it can do in Tasmania, even in the middle of summer. Sofie rang to say that Nygel wouldn't be coming over. He'd fallen off his bike again and knocked one of his front teeth out. The Cosmos was closed because there was no point in it being open. And Blossom just shut herself up in her studio all morning.

Miranda screwed up the *Mercury* and tried to light the fire in the living room, but even that went out. It was all so totally depressing. A battle between Mr Mega-Bucks-Trust-Me-I'm-Here-to-Help-You Ambrazine and The Girl Most Dumped On, Hippo-Bum Hodge. Who did she honestly think was going to win?

In a mood as bleak as the weather, she went to see if Blossom would like to join her in a good cry.

Rain was lashing against the studio window, but everything else was colour and sparkle and light. Under a big overhead lamp, Blossom's work table was strewn with fabrics and papers, sequins, ribbons, laces and beads. Blossom's bright, frizzy head was bent over something she was cutting out of a piece of green taffeta.

'What's that going to be?' Miranda asked.

Blossom looked up and grinned. 'A mermaid's tail,' she said. 'Remember? Think about mermaids. Believe in mermaids. You were the one who told me.'

Miranda pulled a stool up to the table. In spite of everything going so totally pear-shaped, could she really get her believing back? She picked up a bundle of curly gold gift ribbon. 'This could be good for hair,' she said.

They snipped and stitched and glued at mermaids all day. Just before afternoon tea time Angus turned up under a seriously black umbrella, the closest to being excited they'd ever seen him. He'd spent the day in Hobart at the State Archives and had a big envelope of photocopied stuff that he shook out onto the Taurus table.

'There was a wreck in the bay in eighteen seventy-three,' he told them. 'The ship was the *Cornucopia*, her captain was Horace Horn, and she sailed from Plymouth, Devon.'

Before Miranda could ask, he shook his head at her. 'No

mention of mermaids, I'm afraid. And definitely no survivors. But there's enough here for some background, and I'll write the rest of the story myself.'

Miranda wondered how good he'd be at doing that. Marina's story wasn't the regular kind of *Bugle* stuff. It needed vision and imagination, which weren't the first two things you noticed about Angus.

Blossom, however, was thrilled by his offer. 'Wicked!' she shrieked. She threw her arms round Angus and kissed him. Then she looked as amazed about that as he did.

All of a sudden it was very important for her to dash off to the kitchen to get chamomile tea and carrot cake. And Angus seemed to think that it was just as important that he went with her.

Miranda looked at one of the photocopies lying on the Taurus table, and then wished she hadn't. It was the front page of a newspaper from August 1873. 'Hapless Mariners Perish at Sea', the headline yelled with relish. 'None Survive Ghastly Shipwreck Tragedy.' Underneath was a black-and-white drawing of sailors floundering around in enormous waves, their mouths open, their eyes rolled back and their hands clawing the air.

Miranda knew they'd give her nightmares for sure if she didn't turn them all into laughing, waving mermaids. She just hoped her imagination was up to it.

It was nearly six before Angus got ready to leave, and the rain had almost stopped. When Miranda went out on the veranda with Blossom to see him off, she found herself looking at a bay she hadn't seen before. Instead of its usual colour and sparkle it was wrapped in floating veils of heavy mist.

The whole scene would have been perfect for a Theodelinda story. She could just see the Celtic princess, her face moist with drizzle and tears as she stood on the beach and watched Lord Finnewulf's boat sliding away into the mist.

A boat actually was sliding away into the mist, but it looked more like Jack Brannigan's dinghy.

'What's that?' asked Angus. It seemed a pretty dumb question, and Miranda thought his glasses must have been fogged up. But then she saw that he wasn't pointing at the boat, but at a rock on the beach. She could see it only dimly, but she felt sure it was the one on which Jack Brannigan had been sitting on New Year's Eve. Only now it looked as though somebody else was sitting on it.

For one crazy moment she thought it was Christabel Ambrazine. But sitting alone on a wet rock in the middle of a mist didn't really seem like Christabel's thing.

'Hi there!' called Blossom. The figure neither answered nor moved, so it was certainly snobby enough to be Christabel.

It was a mystery, maybe even a murder mystery. The Corpse

on the Rock? But the *Southern Bugle*'s man on the spot still stood squinting out from the veranda. Miranda wondered what had given him the idea he'd make it as a newsman.

Blossom didn't stop to wonder about anything. Her boots scrunching into the wet sand, she went to have a look. Miranda would have gone with her, but she was still a bit spooked by all those drowning sailors and she didn't especially want to meet a corpse this close to bedtime.

'Hey! Come and look at this!' Blossom would never have sounded so excited about a dead body, so Miranda decided to risk it.

Blossom was standing at the foot of the rock, gazing upwards.

'Look, Mim!' she whispered.

Miranda found herself gazing into a small, pointed face with a wide mouth, upturned nose and laughing eyes. Long tendrils of hair flowed out from under a little peaked cap and swirled around bare shoulders. In fact, everything down to the waist was bare. Then came the tail, shiny and scaly and curved around the rock, with the fin at the end in mid-flip.

It was a mermaid carved out of wood, lovingly and beautifully done, a mermaid straight out of her dreams. And because she was shaped so that she could sit firmly on the rock, high above the tide, she was a mermaid who could stay forever and become a part of the bay.

Miranda remembered a crabby, cranky old man sitting on that same rock when she'd told the mermaid story. And that same crabby, cranky old man was the only one who could have carved this mermaid and rowed her around here in his boat.

'Let's go and thank him,' she said in a voice all trembly with tears.

But Blossom said, 'No, he wouldn't want that. He'd probably chase us off with a stick.'

They heard their names being called through the mist, and then they saw Angus plodding towards them in his city shoes. He wasn't exactly Lord Finnewulf, but at least he'd come to see if they were OK.

When he saw the mermaid, he stopped and stared. He even took his glasses off, wiped them on his handkerchief, and put them back on.

'What d'you know,' he said. 'It's a merrow!'

Miranda didn't know what a merrow was. It sounded like some kind of fish. And that just went to show that, with or without his glasses, Angus didn't see very well.

'It's a mermaid,' she explained patiently.

'I know that,' said Angus. 'I've been researching them too.' Something quite close to a grin appeared on his face. 'A merrow is an Irish mermaid. See the little cap? If this carving was in colour, the cap would be red.'

102

Miranda was impressed. Then she was over the moon. First Jack, and now Angus. The dream was catching on. If they could just get rid of Thrillboats Inc., it might be in there with a chance!

Chapter 15

The fuzzy, half-scared, half-excited feeling started before Miranda woke up. As she dragged herself out of sleep she had to check with herself what the feeling was about. When she remembered, it went from a fuzz to a *boing!* Today was Friday — the day when the town took on Jerome Ambrazine. Everybody had their reasons for doing it. Miranda was doing it for Blossom, the Cosmos Café, and the mermaids. But she'd known Ambrazines all her life, and she knew that they liked to win.

One good thing, the light coming through her bedroom window was bright. They would have protested just as hard in the rain, but she was glad they wouldn't have to.

There was actually water in the shower, too. Another good omen. And when she pulled on the usual pair of baggy cotton pants they seemed even baggier than usual. Either the pants were getting bigger, or her bum was getting less hippo.

Blossom was in the kitchen making pancakes with

blueberries for breakfast. In her skimpy orange crop top, belly-button ring and sarong, she looked totally cool. But from the way she was buzzing around like a blowfly and talking non-stop, Miranda knew that Blossom was feeling the same way she was: excited, but very nervous.

George was running a free taxi service for anyone who needed it. On his first trip he dropped off Zeus, Zephyr and Running Water at the Cosmos Café. Then the Kombi was loaded up with placards, picnic baskets, rugs, hats, beach umbrellas and passengers, and they were off.

Miranda hadn't seen the Robinson place before. It was a huge Federation house in an overgrown garden, and it made her think of a gracious old lady dressed in faded, lacy finery and dozing on the clifftop in the sun. Who on earth would want to blast her awake with discos, bistros, jacuzzis and Thrillboats? Nobody but an Ambrazine.

Down at beach level stood a boathouse the size of the Cosmos Café, with a ramp and a runway going all the way to the water. That was where the protesters were going to do their protesting. The pathway down to the beach was wide and paved and a whole heap better than the one at the Cosmos. But then it would be, wouldn't it?

Blossom had meant her group to be the first there, but they weren't. A young mum from the Barneys had, apparently by herself, put up a big awning with rugs, beanbags, a box of beach toys and an Esky. Now she was sitting outside it under a hat like a mushroom, watching a couple of toddlers build a sandcastle.

'Childcare Centre,' she told them, smiling a gentle smile and holding out her arms for Running Water. Miranda felt like warning her that there was no nappy under his T-shirt. But this woman seemed so cool and dreamy that she probably wouldn't notice if she got piddled on.

Somebody else was early, too. Limping a little bit, shuffling quite a lot, but still managing to look as though he meant business, Jack Brannigan was making his way along the beach. Miranda remembered what Blossom had said about not thanking Jack. But the Judy in her got the better of her and she ran to meet the old man. Then, when she reached him, she didn't know what to do. A hug was out of the question, so she just stood looking at him like an utter dork.

Jack looked back with his usual glower, but at least this time he knew who she was.

'You're the one who put a rocket up Ambrazine,' he told her.

'And you're the one who made the mermaid,' she told him.

He gave a 'So what?' sort of shrug, but Miranda couldn't let it end there. The mermaid Jack had made was not from his own Dreaming, but hers. She wanted to let him know that that made the gift even more special.

'Blossom told me your great-grandmother was Aboriginal,' she blurted. Then she wished she hadn't.

Jack's shoulders began to shake. His face crumpled, his eyes watered and he started to make a really weird wheezing noise. What had she done? Was the old man crying, or was he having some kind of a fit?

Slowly it dawned on her that he was laughing. He wiped his eyes with the back of his hand and gave her a grin that was all gappy teeth and bristles. 'Too right she was!' he chortled. 'But my great-grandad was an Irishman!'

They started to walk along to the boatshed together. Miranda told Jack that her own grandmother was a Kelly from Ireland. Jack said he might have known as much.

Miranda thought about Kellys and Brannigans, Celtic princesses and the Aboriginal woman who had married an Irishman. And about all the storytelling and Dreaming there would have to be in that.

Meanwhile, back at the boatshed, they were having a very peaceful protest, so peaceful that some of the protesters had gone to sleep under their beach umbrellas. But that was mainly because there was no sign of Jerome or anyone else from Thrillboats Inc.

'If he's anything like Magnus, he never gets out of bed before nine-thirty,' Blossom told them.

But if Jerome was asleep, he wouldn't be for much longer. With rowdy hymn singing, bongo beating and hallelujahs, the Barneys' bus arrived on the Outing to end all Outings.

The first thing they did was set up a banner that said PEACE ON EARTH – AND THAT MEANS IN OUR BAY! Then Mrs Lovelace made herself comfortable on a couple of cushions slap bang in the middle of the boat ramp. She took out a needle and thread and a piece of patchwork, and looked as though a fleet of battleships wouldn't budge her, let alone one measly Thrillboat.

The ancient Barney was a bit of a worry to begin with. His chair was so wobbly in the sand that it fell over twice, taking him and his bongos with it. But both times he just shouted, 'Praise the Lord!' and didn't seem to mind too much. In the end they borrowed a beanbag from the Childcare Centre and put him in that.

Sofie's idea of what the smart goddess wears to a protest was awesome. She came barefoot down the path in a filmy white dress that floated around her like a cloud. A long white chiffon scarf was tossed around her neck and her hair hung loose to her waist. As if that wasn't enough, over her head she carried a white lace parasol.

'Unreal!' whispered Miranda. It was something else that would have to be put into a book one day.

It was a pity she couldn't say the same about Nygel. He was in his wetsuit again, but today he'd left the stocking off his head. This was obviously so that everyone could see the really gross scabs all over his nose and chin, his fat lip and the gap where his front tooth had been. He seemed to think that a beat-up face did something for his image. But all it said to Miranda was that he should learn to ride his bike properly.

By now there was quite a crowd camped in front of the boatshed. Sunscreen was being rubbed into shoulders and noses, and cold drinks were being passed around. It was all very nice for a day at the beach, but Miranda wondered if people were taking this protest seriously enough. She soon found out.

George came back with another uteload, and then more and more cars started to arrive. Nygel was kept busy handing out placards, but quite a few protesters had brought their own.

One big-bellied man with tattoos, feral chest hair and the spirit of a prize bull seemed to be at the wrong rally. He was brandishing a placard that said NO WAR! and bellowing the same message until he was purple in the face.

This was a job for Blossom's smile, and fearlessly she gave it.

'We do thank you for your support,' she said sweetly. 'But we're not actually here about a war.'

'No,' said the bull. 'But you will be, if Ambrazine don't rack off smartish!'

At that moment Angus turned up with his camera and a placard that said KEEP MARINERS BAY A THRILL-FREE ZONE.

'Is that man threatening Blossom?' he asked Nygel.

'Looks like it,' Nygel said. 'If I were you, I'd thump him one. I'll hold your stuff for you.'

But before Angus had decided whether or not to take up that offer, Blossom patted the bull on his biceps and came scampering over. 'Isn't it fantastic?' she cried happily. 'All these people are on our side!'

It became more fantastic as the morning went on. Not only did the whole of Mariners Bay show up, but half the town without a soul as well. And then some from even further away. But the biggest surprise was when a reporter and a photographer arrived from the *Hobart Mercury*.

What had started out like a beach picnic soon became more like a mardi gras. Guitars strummed, drums throbbed, and somebody had even brought a trumpet. Placard-waving turned to dancing and slogan-chanting to singing. It was party time in the bay.

The Barneys turned themselves into a choir, and with hand-clapping and amazing harmonies gave them some of the good old gospel hymns. Then one of them, a pink-haired lady with earrings the size of ping-pong balls, climbed up to the top of the ramp and sang something called 'I Wish That I Could Shimmy

Like My Sister Kate'. It might not have been a hymn, but it sounded great.

While everybody was clapping and cheering, Blossom muttered in Miranda's ear, 'Don't look now, but the enemy approaches.'

Sure enough, the clapping and cheering turned to howling and booing as down the slope came Jerome, Jason and dear little Christabel.

Chapter 16

They were probably late arriving because it had taken them a long time to decide what to wear to a head-on confrontation with the peasants. All three of them had chosen snazzy sailing outfits in navy blue and white. Jerome was even sporting a yachting cap.

'Is it Regatta Day?' Nygel asked Miranda. 'I'd have put my flippers on if I'd known.'

One thing was for sure, Jerome hadn't expected to see so many people. As he stared at the crowd he looked pretty ropeable. Jason looked pretty uncomfortable and Christabel just looked pretty.

The pink-haired Barney took one look at them and plonked herself down on the ramp next to Mrs Lovelace. Jerome glared at this human barricade and said, between gritted teeth, 'Ladies, would you kindly remove yourselves from my property? Otherwise I shall have you arrested.'

Mrs Lovelace snipped herself a length of blue thread and

the pink-haired Barney gave Jerome a gesture that she hadn't learned in church. They both smiled graciously as the *Mercury* photographer took their photograph.

'I like that woman's spirit,' Jack Brannigan told Miranda, looking admiringly at Mrs Lovelace. 'You wouldn't have her phone number, would yer?'

Jerome was having trouble with his anger management. 'You're all trespassing!' he yelled at the protesters. 'Leave immediately, or I shall call the police!'

'No worries, mate! I'm already here!' Constable Griggs waved a green icypole. 'I'll be on to it the minute things turn nasty.'

But it looked as though the only thing that was going to turn nasty was Jerome. Whipping a remote control out of his blazer pocket, he savagely zapped the boatshed doors. The doors purred upwards and there was the Thrillboat, ready and rearing to go.

Like a Mexican wave at the footy, row after row of protesters sat down. Six or seven deep, they sat on the ramp, they sat on the runway and they sat on the sand. If the Thrillboat was going for a test run today, it would be over quite a few dead bodies.

Miranda, sitting between Sofie and Nygel, wondered what would happen next. As she well knew, Ambrazines aren't easily beaten.

A look of slitty-eyed cunning came over Jerome's face as he planned his next move. Jason Johnston Junior stood hunched up, staring at his rope-soled yachting shoes, and Christabel gazed at the horizon as though it was all too tedious to think about.

'Please don't delude yourselves that you can get the better of me.' Jerome's voice had gone oily again. 'The constable here may not be willing to do his duty, but I'm sure his superiors will be.' He held up his mobile phone. 'You have sixty seconds to disperse. Otherwise I shall call some very senior police officers.'

At first nobody moved. Then somebody did. Christabel began walking down the ramp.

'Don't go down there, sweetie!' her father called. 'Those are not nice people!'

Christabel kept on walking. She stepped carefully around Mrs Lovelace and onto the beach.

Nobody could have been more gobsmacked than Miranda, but Jerome came pretty close. 'Christabel, come back here!' he shouted. 'Christabel, are you listening to me?'

Apparently not. Over the heads of all the people, Christabel was looking at Miranda, and Miranda was looking back at her. Christabel had gone very pale. Edging her way through the crowd, she stopped at last in front of Miranda.

Miranda shuffled sideways to make a space, and Christobel sat down between her and Nygel.

Christabel didn't say a word. She didn't have to, because what she'd just done said it all.

Nygel had this smirky 'Sucked in, Jerome' look all over his scabby face. But Miranda was looking at Christabel's hands. They were bunched up tightly in her lap, and they were trembling.

Suddenly Miranda understood. Christabel wasn't snooty, she was shy. She wasn't bored, she was nervous. All those blank stares were because she was scared. And never more than she was now.

'Christabel!' Jerome thundered. He wasn't nearly so handsome with his face all twisted up in rage. And he wasn't nearly so charming with little globs of spit flying out of his mouth. 'Get yourself up here this instant!'

Christabel was now quivering all over. Miranda knew the feeling, and for the second time that morning she did what Judy would have done. She took hold of one of Christabel's hands and held it tightly.

'Come here!' Jerome shouted again, as though his daughter was a badly trained dog.

Pulling her hand free, Christabel stood up. For an awful moment Miranda thought she was caving in.

'N - no, Daddy.' Christabel's voice was stuttery but clear. 'Y - you can have m - me arrested. I d - don't care!'

The sound of the roaring cheer that went up left any Thrillboat for dead.

'On yer, Christabel!' said Nygel as she sat down again.

Sofie fished a Hughey McDewey Super Chewy Toffee out of her bag and passed it to Christabel. 'You are a very brave girl,' she said.

The fact that the *Mercury* reporter was writing all this down didn't make Jerome any happier. But the slitty-eyed look was back on his face and the battle continued.

'You may be feeling very pleased with yourselves,' he told the crowd. 'But make no mistake, testing of the Thrillboat will continue and Oceana Park will open next summer!'

All this time Jason Johnston Junior had been doing a not-bad imitation of a stuffed wombat. Now, suddenly, he shoved his hands through his gelled-up hair, and then waved them in the air.

'Heck, no, man!' he cried. 'I've had it, Jerry. I quit!'

Jerome gawped at Jason as though his partner was speaking a little-known dialect of Outer Mongolia. 'You *what?*' he spluttered, with a whole heap more spittle globs.

Jason was having trouble keeping still. He shuffled around in his yachting shoes and flung his arms out towards the crowd. 'These are great folks, man! Can't you see what they're doing? They're fighting for what they believe in!'

'So am I!' howled Jerome. 'I believe in the Thrillboat.

Your Thrillboat. Don't *you* believe in it, for Pete's sake?'

Jason looked as if he was about to burst into tears. And that was when Miranda knew that Jerome had stuffed up big time. He'd gone into business with a decent, caring human being.

'Sure I believe in it,' Jason answered at last. 'But this isn't the place for it, Jerry. Even your little Chrissie Bell here can see that.'

At the tops of their voices, two hundred protesters agreed that little Chrissie Bell had got the picture and Jason wasn't wrong.

'Do you mind?' yelled Jerome. 'This is a private conversation!'

They all shut up and listened hard. Actually, it wasn't all that difficult to get the drift of the private conversation. Jerome spoke to Jason as though his partner was a total half-wit and deaf into the bargain.

'Do you remember, Jason?' he asked. 'Do you remember what we said? We said that this place was a gold mine waiting to be discovered. We said that somebody ought to get in quick. And we said that we would be that somebody, didn't we?' He put his arm around Jason's shoulder. 'And do you remember, buddy of mine, that I told you we would make lots and lots of lovely *monee*?'

All this sent Jason back into stuffed wombat mode. Everyone

waited with bated breath to see if he would come out of it. After a long time he blinked hard and licked his lips. In another Mexican wave, the crowd leaned eagerly forward.

'We were wrong,' Jason said. 'Thrillboats in Mariners Bay would be like poker machines in a cathedral. You can take my boats to Sydney. You can take 'em to Surfers. You can take 'em to Lake Chickeepopo for all I care. But you're not having 'em here.'

For a second it looked as if Jerome was going to chuck his biggest whammy of the day. He snatched his arm from Jason's shoulder and opened his mouth to bellow. Then all the bluster leaked out of him like air from a punctured airbed and he stared at his partner. 'Lake *where?*' he asked.

'Chickeepopo,' said Jason. 'Lake Chickeepopo, Wyoming, USA. My home town. Nothing there but the lake, the mountains and the pine forests. Scenery straight from heaven, but man, so boring. I couldn't wait to get outta there.'

It took a lot to flabbergast an Ambrazine, but Jason had managed it without even trying.

'We were months, *months*, looking for somewhere exactly like that!' croaked Jerome. 'Somewhere unknown that *we* could put on the map. And all the time . . . You never said . . . And in *America*, for Pete's sake!'

He put his arm back around Jason's shoulder and gave him

118

a fatherly smile. 'You must tell me more about this Lake Chickiploplop,' he said. 'Real estate would be pretty cheap there in the backwoods, wouldn't it?'

Gently he began to lead the young man back up the path. His voice still drifted down to the beach. 'And this poker machine idea of yours. I like it! I like it! Would there be a cathedral any-where near Lake Chickenpoopoo?'

The protesters sat on the beach, totally forgotten by Jerome Ambrazine. The Thrillboat was left to stare glassily out of its shed.

'He's even forgotten me,' Christabel whispered to Miranda. But she didn't sound too upset about it.

'Far out!' Nygel scowled. 'Is that it, then?' Obviously he'd expected a lot more in the way of abuse-hurling and placard-bashing before the protest was over.

'Did we win?' asked Sofie. Nobody seemed quite sure about that. Then there was another cry of 'Praise the Lord!' and the bongos began their wild beat. So the crowd decided to celebrate, just in case they had won. It was party time again, and as the dancing broke out, Miranda saw Jack Brannigan clambering eagerly up the ramp towards Mrs Lovelace.

This time Blossom didn't join in the revelry. 'I don't trust Jerome Ambrazine,' she said. 'How do we find out what's going on?'

It was Angus who pointed out that they had to give Christabel back.

'N - no, you don't,' said Christabel. 'It'll be ages b - before he remembers me.' She was getting braver by the minute, and was in no hurry to go home.

But Angus insisted that somebody had to get into the house and find out what Jerome was up to. 'You're his ex-second-cousin-in-law,' he told Blossom. 'So I think it should be you. Just take Christabel with you and say you dropped in for a cuppa or something.'

Christabel edged closer to Miranda. 'I w - want you to come, too,' she said.

And as Miranda's father was Christabel's ex-second-cousin-in-law, she decided that perhaps she'd better.

Chapter 17

Miranda lay in bed and thought about the day she'd just had. For a Friday in Mariners Bay it had been pretty awesome.

Christabel had taken them up to the house and they'd found Jerome in the gigantic lounge room going ballistic on the Internet. He was onto the Community Online Centre in Lake Chickeepopo, and somebody had gone across the street to fetch Jason's gran, because she had some photos that Jerome could look at.

This was one very excited Jerome Ambrazine. 'Hello, my angel poppet!' He blew a vague kiss at Miranda. 'How's Daddy's little girl?'

Blossom opened her mouth to give him heaps, but Christabel said, 'It's OK. He's got things on his m - mind.'

Jerome certainly had. 'Jason!' he hooted. 'This could be the big one! This could be the jackpot! Chickenpoo could make Mariners Bay look like chickenfeed!'

He gazed intently at the screen as the photos started coming through. There didn't seem to be much chance of a cuppa, so Blossom and Miranda moved in to take a closer look.

The first picture was of Jason, aged about two, wearing nothing but a droopy nappy and sucking his thumb.

'Oh, cute!' cried Blossom.

Jason turned the colour of a ripe tomato and put his hands over the screen.

'Are you sure your gran knows what we want?' Jerome sounded just a bit edgy. 'I didn't ask for the family album.'

Jason bent and peered through his fingers, and then took his hands away. And even Miranda, who thought that Mariners Bay was the most fabulous place on earth, was absolutely rapt when she saw the picture on the screen.

It was the kind of scene you see on one of those calendars that the butcher gives away free at Christmas, or on a gift box of Hughey McDewey Super Chewy Toffees. Lake Chickeepopo was all dazzling water, towering pine trees and snow-capped purple mountains – nearly too beautiful to be true.

As photo after photo flashed up, Jerome actually started to foam at the mouth. Through frothy bubbles of greed he gabbled, 'Christabel, sweetie, you're going to have to go home to Mummy. Daddy and Jason have to go to America on business!'

Christabel looked at Miranda. Then she took a deep breath and said, 'N - no, D - Daddy. I don't want to go home. I w - want to stay here.'

Jerome obviously didn't know what he'd done to deserve such a tiresome child. 'You can't stay here by yourself,' he snapped. 'And Daddy is going away.'

Christabel had already thought that one out. 'Mummy c - can come here,' she said. 'We can stay here t - together. It's only for three more weeks.'

Poor Jerome. He was just an ordinary bloke trying to make a few million dollars the only way he knew how. Why did people have to make it so difficult?

'Mummy's not well,' he said, his eyes still on the screen. 'She wouldn't like it here. Now please stop arguing with Daddy.'

'Argue,' whispered Blossom. 'Go on, argue!'

Christabel nodded, and took another deep breath. 'She would like it,' she said. 'It w - would do her good.'

Not bad, but now Christabel needed some back-up. 'Send for her mother,' said Blossom. 'Christabel can stay with us until she comes.' Then she added, 'Or even if she doesn't come.'

Christabel at the Cosmos? While both the girls were thinking about that one, Jerome flapped his hand at Blossom without even looking at her. 'OK, OK,' he grunted.

And that was how Miranda came to be lying in her room

with Christabel sleeping on a camp bed only a couple of metres away. Only she couldn't have been sleeping, because the next minute she whispered, 'M - Mim, are you sure you don't mind me being here?' Which just went to show that, as arrogant Ambrazines go, Christabel was an absolute zero.

'Course not,' Miranda whispered back. 'As soon as your mother gets your email she'll come for sure.' Then she asked something that she'd been wondering about. 'What kind of not well is she?'

There was a silence, then Christabel said, 'She – she gets depressed. It hurt her a lot when D - Daddy left. I guess she felt like a reject.'

Miranda said, 'Oh, right,' because she couldn't think of anything else to say. She fell asleep wondering how many Ambrazine rejects there were in the world.

Ever since Miranda had met Christabel she'd been putting her in the same basket as Jacinta Jacques. But Friday had been full of surprises, and on Saturday there were more to come. The two of them were having breakfast on the veranda when Christabel suddenly said, 'I w - wish I could be like you.'

Miranda nearly choked on a mouthful of muesli. What was it Christabel wanted? A big bottom? Wobbly thighs? Braces on her teeth? Or all of the above?

'You're always d - doing stuff,' Christabel told her. 'Really c - cool stuff that you w - want to do. And when you stood up at that m - meeting and told my father you were going to fight him, I thought you were so b - brave.'

Oh, that. Miranda knew she'd have to tell the truth. 'That wasn't me,' she said. 'That was somebody I made up.'

Christabel stared at her with wide blue eyes. 'You – you've got somebody else inside you?' she asked. 'So have I. B - but she never gets out.'

'Theodelinda isn't supposed to,' said Miranda. 'But some-times she does.' Then she said, 'And anyway, somebody who looks a lot like you was pretty brave yesterday.'

From then on it was a lot easier to tell Christabel about the mermaids. So she explained her idea that thinking, dreaming and wishing about mermaids could make them real.

'It could even bring mermaids back to the bay,' she said, hoping that Christabel wouldn't think she was completely crazy.

Christabel thought hard for a moment and then said, 'W - well, it could work. When I was l - little I wanted a unicorn for Christmas. I just b - believed and b - believed that I was going to get one, and in the end I got a white p - pony. So I was close!'

Well, as close as her father could get, thought Miranda. Wishing and dreaming must be a lot easier if you know you can have just about anything you want. If there'd been a unicorn for sale, Jerome would have bought it.

She looked at the bay sparkling peacefully in the sun. The Thrillboat wouldn't be out there today, but neither were the swans. Perhaps the swans were gone forever, and mermaid dreaming was a really dumb idea. This morning there was even something a bit lonely and sad about Jack's little merrow, sitting on her rock and waiting for something that wasn't going to happen.

It was ages since Miranda had had a Podge moment, but she could feel one coming on now. She could almost hear Jacinta Jacques saying, 'Mermaids? Trust me, Podgy Hodge, you're a dag!'

What she actually did hear was Christabel saying, 'I c - could draw some m - mermaids. Would that help?'

Miranda smiled at her. 'Yes,' she said. 'That would help a lot.'

Then George's ute pulled up and Zephyr came racing down the path with her bare feet flapping and her Native Indian beads bouncing as she waved a fat *Saturday Mercury* over her head.

'We won! We won!' she yelled. So much for her sixth sense if she had to wait to read that in the newspaper. But her excited cries brought out Blossom, who grabbed the paper from her.

'Greenies Stitch Up Resort Tycoon' was how the *Mercury* put it. And there on the front page was a photo of Mrs Lovelace doing her patchwork on the boat ramp.

'She doesn't exactly look like a g - greenie,' said Christabel.

'Down here, anybody who protests is a greenie,' Blossom told her.

The *Mercury* article wouldn't have pleased Jerome much, but he probably hadn't seen it. As far as anyone knew, he and Jason were on the first flight available to Melbourne. And from there it was straight to the USA and li'l ol', lucky ol' Lake Chickeepopo.

'I wonder what he'll do with the Robinson place,' said Miranda. 'Sell it, I suppose.'

And then Christabel came out with another of her off-the-planet specials. 'I'm going to ask him to g - give it to me.'

Miranda usually tried not to gape, because with her braces it wasn't a good look. But right now she gaped. How could a thirteen-year-old own a house?

'He can put it in trust with M - Mummy until I'm old enough,' Christabel said. 'If I ask him to, he w - will.'

Miranda turned her gape on Blossom, who nodded. 'He probably will,' she said.

At this point Nygel showed up on his bike. Without a motor-bike magazine to distract him, he was able to focus his mind on Christabel. Naturally he had to give her his streetfighter spiel, and she seemed suitably impressed. But it was a pity that the Mangler's face still looked as though the last fight he'd been in he'd lost.

The three of them went to sit under the merrow rock to do some serious mermaid dreaming, but Nygel's mind wasn't on the job. He might have looked like an emu, but this morning he had more attitude than a peacock. Swaggering down the veranda steps, he'd pulled his stomach in so far that Miranda thought his bathers would fall down. His chest, on the other hand, was puffed out as far as it would go, which wasn't very far. He actually said to Christabel, 'May I?' and took her towel and spread it out for her to sit on. It would have been positively puke-making if it hadn't been so funny. But Christabel treated it all as normal, which it probably was for her.

Miranda sighed as she spread out her own towel. It didn't look as if Nygel was going to do any more wishing for mermaids. Clearly he thought he'd found one.

Chapter 18

Willow Ambrazine, Christabel's mother, was supposed to arrive on Monday afternoon. She was coming over on the ferry and then driving down from Devonport. The plan was that she'd pick up Christabel from the Cosmos, and then, with Jerome safely on the other side of the planet, they'd both go and stay at the Robinson place.

Miranda knew that Christabel was scared stiff that the depression thing would stop her mother from coming. Not that she said so, but all weekend she grew quieter and quieter. Most of the time she sat with her sketchbook doing coloured pencil drawings of mermaids. The mermaids she drew were very much like the ones that Miranda pictured in her mind, which was utterly amazing really.

An hour before Willow was due to arrive at the Cosmos, Christabel went up to the car park to wait for her. Miranda hung about in the garden, trying to think mermaids, picking strawberries for afternoon tea and praying that, for Christabel's sake, Willow would turn up.

And Willow did. Her silver car hummed into the car park so quietly that Blossom, who was used to listening for vehicles that rattled and burped, nearly missed it. But something must have told her, because the flyscreen slammed and she was out there with Miranda to watch as Willow walked down the path with Christabel.

As soon as Miranda saw Willow, she felt all blubber and braces. Christabel's mother was blonde and slim and gorgeous, and just so elegant in her white linen pantsuit and thin gold chains. But there was a kind of droopy look about her, and she peered out from behind her silky fair hair with the wary eyes of the severely dumped on.

'Weeping Willow,' sighed Blossom.

Miranda had been thinking of a frightened rabbit, but a weeping willow was certainly more poetical.

One thing was for sure, Christabel loved her mother heaps. She wasn't the kind to go crazy with excitement, but there was a shine about her that hadn't been there before Willow arrived.

When they took her into the house, Willow seemed to be looking for the nearest dark cupboard to crawl into. They got her into the living room and sat her on a saggy couch with a glass of fresh apple juice in front of her and Christabel beside her. Then, to fill any awkward silences, Blossom gave a twenty-minute talk on 'My Life Without Magnus So Far'. It was meant to say to Willow, 'If I can survive the Ambrazines, so can you.' So she missed out the bits about the Cosmos being a total flop and bankruptcy staring her in the face.

When she'd run out of amazing things to say about an Ambrazine-free life, she said brightly to Willow, 'What do you do, then?'

Willow said, 'Nothing much.'

But Christabel said, 'M - Mummy used to design jewellery.'

Blossom jumped on that. 'Really?' she cried. 'How absolutely fascinating!'

But Willow said, 'I don't any more,' and that was the end of that conversation.

No offence to Christabel, but Miranda was beginning to think that Weeping Willow was the most boring person she'd ever met. She just sat there, gazing around the room as if she was looking for a way to escape.

But anyone who gazed around Blossom's living room was in for a few surprises. They saw Willow stare at the griffin hatching out in the fireplace, and not long after that she came eyeball to eyeball with the troll on top of the bookcase. Not that she said anything – that would have been too much to expect.

But the strained look on her face did ease up a bit, so Blossom moved in fast.

'This place does bring out the whacky bits in you,' she laughed. 'Wait till you see the café!'

Miranda doubted that Willow had any whacky bits, but she got the tour of the Cosmos anyway. She still didn't say much, but she stared a lot, which was what most people did. Then, getting desperate by now, Blossom took Willow into her studio.

Between them Blossom and Miranda had made about a dozen mermaids, and Christabel's drawings were tacked up on the wall. Willow's cheeks actually turned a little bit pink. She gazed and gazed, and reached out ever so gently to touch. It was as if she could hardly believe what she was seeing and touching.

Miranda didn't dare to tell her about the mermaid dreaming in case she thought that Christabel had got in with a bunch of utter nutters, but Christabel told her all about it anyway. Willow listened with a serious face, and all she said was, 'I see.'

Soon after that, they left. Willow knocked back an offer of strawberries and cream and thanked them politely for looking after Christabel. They'd been very kind, she said. She didn't say anything else, and Miranda had no way of knowing when she'd see Christabel again.

Christabel had only camped in her room for three nights, so

Miranda shouldn't really have missed her, but she did. It took her ages to get to sleep that night. Then, when she did, a piercing scream from Blossom's room suddenly woke her up again.

It was one of those heart-thumping, sweaty moments when it's hard to decide what to do. Hide under the doona? Rush to the rescue? Or scream back? Just as she'd decided to run and scream at the same time, her bedroom door burst open and the light flicked on.

Wild-eyed and wild-haired, Blossom stood there in the extra-large man's shirt she wore to bed. Her face was pale green and slimy, but Miranda realised that was only her home-made avocado-and-spinach night cream.

'Mim!' Blossom shrieked. 'It's just come to me! Do you know who she is?'

It was a tough question. 'Who who is?' Miranda knew she sounded like an owl, but she couldn't help it.

'She's Willow Hampton. That's who!' Blossom threw herself down on the end of the bed. 'You know! Willow Hampton!'

Miranda didn't know, not really. But she guessed Blossom was talking about Weeping Willow, who didn't really seem exciting enough to get people rushing around and screaming in the middle of the night.

But that was where Miranda was wrong.

Years ago, Blossom told her, Willow Hampton jewellery

had been jewellery to die for – not because it was super ritzy glitzy, but because it was somehow out of this world.

'I mean that!' Blossom said. 'Willow Hampton had her own special magic. But it was a rare kind of magic, and a rare kind of jewellery she put it into. Heaps of people wanted it, but you couldn't just walk into a shop and buy it. You had to have it specially made.'

'And that's Christabel's mother?' gasped Miranda. 'Droopy old Weeping Willow?'

'Was,' Blossom said. 'She was always a bit of a mystery woman. Nobody really knew who she was. Then, about ten years ago, Willow Hampton jewellery stopped happening. And when the magic disappeared, she just got forgotten.'

'That'd be right,' Miranda agreed, thinking of forgotten mermaids. 'But how come you're so sure that Christabel's mum is her?'

Blossom's eyes shone out of her gunky green face. 'Don't things just come to you, *boing*, when you're nearly asleep? Christabel said that her mum used to design jewellery. And then I realised that that's what it is about Christabel's mermaids. She's got her mother's magic!'

Miranda knew she was right. But there was just one more question. 'Magnus never told you that Jerome was once married to Willow Hampton?'

Blossom gave a loud snort. 'Ambrazines have enough trouble keeping track of who they've been married to themselves. Never mind all the rest of the family.'

Well. The two of them sat and looked at each other.

'I don't think Christabel's mum would want us to tell anyone who she is,' said Miranda.

'Just what I was thinking,' said Blossom. 'So we won't.'

Chapter 19

Tuesday didn't look like being such a good day. Christabel didn't call. Nygel had to go to a dentist in Hobart to see about a new tooth, and Blossom was going up to Celestial Supplies for some more disgustingly wholesome stuff for the Cosmos, so she said she'd take him. Miranda could have gone with them, and she nearly did. But with everything that had been going on, the mermaid dreaming seemed to be slipping a bit and she knew she ought to get it up and running again. So she stayed at the Cosmos. And as it turned out, she was glad she did.

As soon as Zeus and Zephyr arrived, things started to improve. Zephyr had an idea for making seaweed muffins more appealing by chucking some honey and chopped gherkins into the recipe. 'They'll still be green,' she admitted. 'But if we call them mermaid muffins, that'll be understandable.'

With Running Water slung on her back in a shawl, she set to work to reinvent the muffin. Miranda set herself up at the bench and got just as busy trying to turn a couple of seashells into a bra. Not for herself, but for a little mermaid she'd made out of driftwood.

But the best thing was that Zeus had written a mermaid song. It was called 'Song for Marina', and it was just so beautiful.

Zeus taught them to sing it so that their voices made a really cool echoing sound. It was like the wind in the rigging of a tall ship, or mermaids singing in a coral cave. Once they got into it they didn't want to stop, so they flowed their song round and round the kitchen while they got on with what they had to do.

If there was one thing rarer than mermaids, it was paying customers at the Cosmos Café. That was why none of them took much notice when a knocking sound started up as a kind of backing to their song. Miranda thought it might have been the phantom possum.

But a possum doesn't usually yell 'Shop!' at the top of its voice. So they stopped their singing in the middle of a verse and listened. There was definitely somebody on the other side of the bead curtain. Possibly somebody who wanted to be served.

'About time!' growled Jack Brannigan as the entire staff rattled through the curtain at once. At least, they thought it was Jack. He was sitting on one of the high stools at the counter in a pink shirt with a big stiff collar and an even bigger green-and-yellow striped tie. His hair was neatly parted in the middle and plastered down on each side of his head with some kind of grease that smelled of violets. And he'd actually had a shave of sorts.

Beside him sat Mrs Lovelace. She was wearing a blue flowered dress, pink lipstick and a blue chiffon scarf tied round her hair with a bow on top.

'Don't mind him,' Mrs Lovelace said. 'The singing was lovely. I could have listened all day.'

'I thought we were going to have to,' grunted Jack. 'But when I take a lady out, I expect service first and the entertainment after.'

Going out? Jack and Mrs Lovelace? Even Miranda's imagination had never stretched that far.

Mrs Lovelace looked at their faces and smiled. 'That's right, my dears,' she said. 'We are on a date. Our first, as it happens.'

Miranda felt sure it was the café's first first date. But they could handle it. Zephyr untied Running Water and handed him to Miranda. 'We have a window table for two that is vacant,' she told the happy couple. 'Please come this way.'

Zeus grabbed a menu and raced after them. 'Thank you for choosing the Cosmos,' he said. 'May I recommend the mermaid muffins? Fresh from the oven and ready to melt in your mouth.' Then he grabbed his guitar and began to sing 'Love is in the Air'.

Jack had trouble believing that they called themselves a café, but had no meat pies, no sausage rolls, and no chips, with or without gravy. Miranda dreaded what he would think of mermaid muffins.

He thought they were brilliant. He said his Auntie Doris used to make exactly the same muffins for him when he was a kid, which was pretty amazing considering that Zephyr had only invented the recipe that morning. Mrs Lovelace had never come across a mermaid muffin before and didn't seem all that thrilled that she had now. So she had carrot cake and orange juice while Jack ate five muffins washed down with a pot of nasturtium tea.

While Jack was in such a good mood, Miranda sat down at their table with Running Water and told them all about her plan to dream mermaids back to the bay. She knew they'd understand what she was talking about, and they did.

'Oh, I could do that, dear!' Mrs Lovelace's eyes shone at the very idea.

Jack wet his finger and mopped up the last few crumbs from his plate. 'You know what?' he said thoughtfully. 'The best time for that kind of thing is at sunset. Just when day's turning into night. You'd be surprised what can happen round about then.'

There was only one way to find out. So they arranged to meet at the Cosmos in time for sunset tomorrow.

When tomorrow came, Miranda didn't have to wait until sunset to be surprised. Nygel arrived on his bike at about ten o'clock in the morning. His new tooth wasn't in yet, but his gap was the only thing that Miranda and Blossom recognised. No more daggy jeans and murderous T-shirt. Nygel wore tight black pants with a cummerbund, high-heeled boots, a white shirt with ruffles down the front and a bandanna round his stubbled head.

'Christabel's not here,' Miranda said. 'She's at the Robinson place with her mother.'

Nygel said, 'Oh, right,' and swung his leg back over the saddle to ride off. It would have looked really cool if his pants hadn't split.

Blossom grabbed his handlebars. 'Christabel and her mother are having some quality time together, you know.'

But Miranda remembered that Nygel wouldn't know. Not about things like that. 'Why don't you hang with me?' she offered. 'I've got a new song I can teach you. Plus some really hot gossip about who's dating who. Plus something utterly amazing could be happening here tonight.'

Nygel wasn't impressed. He screwed his face into a sneer and his bandanna fell over his eyes.

'Your bathers are in the bathroom where you left them,' Blossom told him. 'Give me your pants and I'll mend them.'

Nygel didn't have much choice, and Blossom certainly took her time getting round to fixing his pants. Like all day.

Miranda decided that having friends could be hard work. She had two of them now, but Christabel had disappeared off the planet and Nygel was being harder to get on with than Jacinta Jacques when she had a pimple on her chin and only came second in maths. Ah well. She sang the mermaid song to him and told him about Jack Brannigan and Mrs Lovelace. And she let him beat her in a swimming race, even though that meant she had to dog-paddle on the spot.

Blossom had brought home a Celestial Supplies freebie calendar which told them that the sun would set that night at half past eight. George dropped Zephyr, Zeus and Running Water off at six-thirty. At seven o'clock Jack and Mrs Lovelace came walking along the beach hand in hand. They were both barefoot and she was wearing a soft, drifting kind of dress in palest lavender. It made her look very young.

As soon as Nygel found out they were all there for a mega mermaid dreaming, he said it was time he got going. But then Blossom started serving up her special brown rice and eggplant bake. For something so good for you, it didn't taste bad at all. So Nygel stayed and had three helpings, just to be polite.

Jack said they wouldn't want to know what health foods did

to his stomach. 'Give me them good old-fashioned muffins like auntie used to make,' he said. So they did.

'What are we going to do until sunset, then?' Nygel wanted to know.

Miranda had been thinking about that all day. 'A sand sculpture,' she said. 'We could make a giant mermaid on the beach.'

'Far out!' snorted Nygel. 'How exciting is that?'

'You can mind Running Water,' Zephyr told him. But Nygel thought his pants had been through enough for one day, and he knocked back her offer. That didn't matter, though, because Running Water was happy enough rolling round on a rug and eating sand, just as long as he was part of things.

Blossom conjured up a collection of spades, trowels and even big serving spoons for mermaid sculpting, and they all went down to the beach. They agreed that their mermaid needed to be big, at least three metres long. And something told them that she needed to be just above the waterline, so that the next tide would gently wash her into the sea.

Miranda wasn't especially artistic, she knew that. She could only use words to describe the pictures in her head. But between them Blossom and Jack were able to get everyone working on a mermaid that was as beautiful as anything Miranda could have imagined.

The sun was low in the sky and everything shone like polished glass. Even the far-off hills that Miranda shared a spirit with were sharp and clear, and the sound of voices and laughter was carried on the still air.

Miranda wandered off by herself and began to gather up trailing fronds of emerald and scarlet seaweed. There was something on her mind. No matter how many times she pushed it out, it kept creeping back. It was time – something that never seemed to matter much in this place. But for Miranda it was running out. She had just two weeks left in Mariners Bay. Two weeks to make the dreaming come true and to do for Blossom what she'd promised to do. Something had to happen, and it had to happen soon. Like tonight. Please, *please* let something happen tonight.

She looked towards the sea, and the late sunlight hit the water with a brilliance that dazzled her. Magic! Blossom, with the light behind her, was a dancing shadow that waved and called to her. So she ran back to them with her gorgeous mermaid decorations.

Blossom finished off the mermaid with long, flowing locks of green and red hair. A bit punk, perhaps, but absolutely fabulous and absolutely right.

The sun was only just above the horizon now and everything had a pinkish sort of glow. They sat on the sand and gazed at their mermaid, feeling the stillness and knowing that this was definitely a time when anything could happen.

'Do you know what?' Mrs Lovelace said. 'I think this calls for a liturgical dance.' She stood up and shook out the soft folds of her dress. Zeus began to strum on his guitar the opening chords of 'Song for Marina'.

'Have you got a dance for mermaids?' Miranda asked Jack.

'We've got a dance for everything,' he said as he got himself to his feet.

Then they all began to sing. And as 'Song for Marina' echoed across the sea, an old woman and an old man, like the Owl and the Pussycat, danced hand in hand on the edge of the sand.

As the sun slid over the edge of the earth, a new sound came into their song. It was the steady beating of wings. Across a sky streaked with crimson and gold, seven black swans flew out of the sunset and swooped down to settle in the waters of the bay.

Chapter 20

On Thursday Australia's slackest newspaper, the *Southern Bugle*, reappeared after its Christmas break. Zephyr brought it to work with her and Miranda grabbed it eagerly. After all, a lot of stuff had happened in the past couple of weeks.

The whole of the front page was taken up with a very serious crime. Some time between Christmas and New Year someone had stolen a blow-up plastic Santa from the roof of the mayor's house. The mayor and mayoress had been away enjoying a well-earned rest at their holiday shack when the thief struck.

'"That Santa has been on our roof every Christmas for the past thirty years," the distraught mayoress sobbed yesterday. "What kind of person would do such a terrible thing?"'

Miranda stopped reading and stared at Blossom and Zephyr over the top of the paper. 'Angus didn't write this, did he?' she asked fearfully.

'No,' said Blossom. 'That'd be Carmel Bracebridge, their crime and cookery writer.'

That was a relief, because Ms Bracebridge went on to say that the criminal could well strike again. 'Grave fears are held for garden gnomes, fairy lights, wishing wells and other treasured items that mean so much to our community,' she had written.

What about the protest? Miranda flicked through the paper and found it in the middle.

Angus's report had been cut down to three paragraphs to make room for the results of the Brownies' Grand New Year Raffle, but there was a photograph of Jerome looking as though he was having some kind of fit. 'Mr Ambrazine addressing the rally,' the caption read.

Then, on the second-last page of the *Bugle*, Miranda found something that knocked her socks off: 'Once There Were Mermaids', a Special Feature by Angus Bloom. Beneath it was a picture of the merrow seated on her rock. And as Miranda began to read, she realised one thing for sure. Angus was a terrific writer.

He wrote that Mariners Bay had once been Marina's Bay, and told the whole story of Marina and Captain Hornpipe, the shipwreck and the mermaids in the bay. And he told it in a way that made it seem very likely to be true.

'A hundred years ago, people saw mermaids in the bay,' Angus wrote. 'They believed that the mermaids were there, and they expected to glimpse them from time to time. And so, of course, they did.'

Exactly right, Miranda thought. She moved on to the last paragraph.

'Once there were mermaids in our bay. Could there be mermaids again?'

Then she saw it! Aargh!

'One person who believes that there could be is thirteen-year-old Miranda Hodge, currently staying at the Cosmos Café. For Miranda it is all a matter of faith. "If people believe hard enough, it will happen," she says.'

Angus went on to explain how Miranda 'and some friends' were mermaid believing and mermaid dreaming for all they were worth in the hope that once again there would be mermaids in the bay.

How embarrassing! Mermaid believing was OK to share with a few special people. But there were a whole heap more people out there who would read that and think that thirteen-year-old Miranda Hodge was a little weird, to say the least.

Blossom didn't see that as a problem. 'They think we're all fruit-loops down here anyway,' she said.

'Where on earth did this weather come from?' Zephyr wanted to know. The sky outside the kitchen window was as black as the inside of a cow at midnight. Blossom turned on the light so that she could see to read Angus's story and the rain started to drum down on the roof.

That was the start of a downer that went on for days. It was cold, it was wet, and any magic that might have been hanging around from the night before seemed to have gone down the gurgler with the rain.

Miranda tried. She kept turning her mind back to that enchanted moment when the black swans flew in out of the sunset. Jack had told her that some people had once believed that mermaids could take on the form of swans. So maybe that was it. Maybe the swans' return was the answer to all the believing and dreaming. But if they didn't look like mermaids, they weren't much help to Blossom, or the Cosmos.

Surprise, surprise, there wasn't a single customer all day. Blossom cleaned the stove and Zephyr defrosted the fridge. Miranda went to her room and dug her Theodelinda story out of her suitcase. A fat lot of good that did. Theodelinda had been under the bed for weeks and seemed to want to stay there. So Miranda chewed her pen and stared at a blank page until Blossom called her because Christabel was on the phone.

All Christabel told her was that she and her mum were really busy, which was nice for them. 'We'll see you soon,' she said. But she didn't say when. It was only after she'd hung up that Miranda realised that Christabel hadn't stammered once.

The worst thing happened when it was time for Zephyr to go home. They could hear George beeping his horn, and Blossom had her pay all ready in an envelope. But as Zephyr took it, she gave Blossom a long, kind, sad look.

'I think today's the day we have to face it, Bloss,' she said. 'You can't afford to keep on giving me this, can you?'

Miranda didn't know if this was sixth sense or just common sense. But she knew it was true.

Blossom gulped and even her freckles seemed to have gone pale. 'Oh, Zeph!' she wailed. 'What are we going to do?'

Zephyr put her pay envelope down on the bench. 'We're going to go on being friends, that's what,' she said. 'But I'm not taking any more of your money, and neither is Zeus. We've talked about it, and he feels the same way I do.' Then she gave Blossom a real Judy-style hug. 'Friends, OK?' she said again. And she was out of the door and racing through the rain before Blossom could say another word.

Miranda slumped onto a stool. This wasn't the way things were supposed to go. 'I tried, Blossom,' she said hopelessly. 'I really did.'

It seemed like a good time for some serious howling. But Blossom wasn't ready for that. She was still pale, and her voice was shaky, but she was hanging in there.

'We've all tried,' she said. 'So let's go and try some more.'

And that's how they came to finish up the day down in the studio. Miranda kept telling herself that stitching green sequins onto a calico mermaid wasn't a waste of time. But who was she kidding?

On Saturday it rained all day. Blossom had the brilliant idea that if they stayed in bed hordes of customers would come battering at the door. But that didn't work, so at ten o'clock they got up.

They did some more work on mermaids, played Scrabble and baked yet another carrot cake.

'Good fun, isn't it?' Blossom kept saying a bit too brightly. 'Just the two of us, doing whatever we like.'

As hard as she tried, Miranda couldn't get the voice in her head to shut up. 'You might as well pack your bags and go home right now,' the voice kept saying. 'It's the same old story, Hippo-Bum Hodge. You're a loser!'

On Sunday it rained again, and even Blossom started to run out of steam. It was so chilly that they lit the fire in the living room and curled up on beanbags in front of it. Blossom started to check through the newspaper for part-time jobs she might be able to apply for, before she noticed that the paper was two months old.

Miranda had another go at her Theodelinda story, but her Writer's Block was still jammed solid.

Then, amazingly, three people arrived at the Cosmos for lunch. This would have been a major breakthrough if the three people hadn't been Sofie, Nygel and Angus.

All the same, they sat at the Taurus table and ordered from the menu just like real customers. The only difference was that Blossom and Miranda ate with them and Blossom wouldn't let them pay.

'You're guests,' she said. 'Practically family.'

When Angus opened his wallet she slapped it closed again. 'That story you wrote was wonderful, just wonderful!' she cried. 'We owe you more than Sunday lunch!' Then she burst into tears.

For a second everyone just sat there. Then Sofie took charge, clucking gentle things in Greek and offering a little white lace handkerchief.

But this was a job for more than a lace handkerchief. Blossom bawled and blubbered and snuffled, and tried to talk at the same time. What came out wasn't much easier to under-stand than Sofie's Greek, but it was along the lines that she, Blossom, was a half-baked lunatic to think she could run a business. The Cosmos was a king-sized bummer, the staff had gone, the money had gone and everything was utterly and totally stuffed.

After that she blew her nose on her serviette, wiped her eyes with the back of her hand, took a deep breath and said, 'Sorry about that.'

Nygel sat and blinked. Angus took his glasses off, polished them on *his* serviette and put them on again.

'Blossom,' he said gruffly. 'I've been meaning to talk to you about something. I've decided I'm going to write a book. Folk stories, local yarns and history, that kind of stuff. I'd need the right place to work, and I was wondering if, after Mim goes home, I might rent your spare room. That'd be great for me, and it'd bring you in a bit of money.'

Perhaps Blossom was too upset to know what she was saying, but what she did say was, 'Angus Bloom, you're an angel and I love you!' And while Angus was still all boggle-eyed about that, she added the next bit. 'You can have my spare room for nothing. But I don't know for how long. Because the thing is, I'm going to have to sell this place.'

Sell the Cosmos? Miranda felt sick.

'If I can find anybody dumb enough to buy it, that is!' Blossom tried to laugh, but didn't quite make it.

'My mother would!' This was Nygel. 'She would if I asked her to!'

It was possibly the dopiest thing Miranda had ever heard Nygel say. What would Rhiannon Fayn want with a run-down café on a deserted beach at a place nobody had heard of? But when she turned to Nygel to tell him to get real, she saw that his emu eyes were frantic. Dopey or not, Nygel cared, and he was desperate to help.

'Your mother would not!' Sofie was speaking English again and the goddess fire was in her eyes. 'Because the Cosmos will not be for sale!' She glared at Blossom. 'That serpent you were married to wants to give you money. Take it! Take every cent he has, then twice as much again!'

Blossom glared back and said she'd rather live in a cave and sell clothes pegs door to door for a living.

On and on they talked and argued, trying to find an answer when there wasn't one to be found.

Miranda didn't say anything. She'd had her one idea and it hadn't worked. Everyone who read this week's *Bugle* would know what a nutcase she was. But worse than that was the thought that Blossom's beautiful dream had ended and Miranda would never stay with her at the Cosmos again. She felt as though something or someone had dumped on them from a very great height.

Chapter 21

The next day it stopped raining. The sun came out and the bay got its sparkle back. Blossom tried hard to get hers back, too.

'One thing about total ruin,' she said. 'It leaves you stacks of time for other things.' And she put the 'Closed' sign up on the café door.

Then she dressed herself in a long mauve gown with silver sequins, Sofie's white satin hat and her own bushwalking boots.

'Want to go to Hobart and check out the movies?' she asked.

Miranda didn't, not especially. She could go to the movies back home in Sydney. Or she could when she could afford it. And that was another thing. Could Blossom afford it now? Whatever, Blossom had made up her mind that they were going *somewhere*. So up the path they went to the Kombi.

That was as far as they got. The next thing was that a mini bus swung into the car park and pulled up behind them. Out jumped a young man and a young woman, who opened up the side door and let out a whole mob of little kids. Miranda wasn't sure if the two minders said that these were happy daisies, or if they were in a happy daze. The kids seemed happy enough, but certainly not dazed. A couple of them, about seven years old, were carrying between them something that looked like a giant fish.

'Are you Miranda Hodge?' the female minder wanted to know. Miranda could only admit that she was.

'Right!' the woman beamed. 'This is for you, then.'

The children shyly shoved the fish at Miranda, and she saw that it wasn't a fish at all. It was a papier mâché mermaid, gorgeously crinkled and woolly-haired and painted in brilliant poster paint colours. When Miranda took it, the children all got off-the-planet noisy and excited, as you do when you've made something special for somebody and they really like it.

It was Blossom who managed to sort out that they were the Happy Days School Holiday Club. They'd read about Miranda and her dream of mermaids and decided to do something about it.

Blossom, who already had most of the little girls absolutely ecstatic about her mauve gown and silver sequins, invited them down to the Cosmos. Miranda put her beautiful mermaid on the counter where everyone could see that she was really quite something.

The Happy Dazes thought the Cosmos was quite something, too. The bare lady with her flowering belly button had the kids in hysterics.

Then, while Blossom was up to her eyes serving orange juice and carrot cake, somebody else turned up. She came in very quietly, a tiny woman in a rainbow smock and with amazing silver hair piled on top of her head. She had owlish spectacles on the end of her nose and she was carrying a little parcel wrapped in tissue paper.

'I'm looking for Miranda Hodge,' she said in exactly the soft voice you'd expect her to have.

'That's me,' said Miranda. The woman put her parcel down on the Gemini table and gave her the sweetest smile. 'I am Helga,' she said as she carefully unwrapped the tissue paper. 'And I want to give you this.'

'This' was a ceramic mermaid no bigger than Miranda's little finger. It was so tiny and delicate that she was almost afraid to breathe on it. 'Oh,' she whispered as she gazed at the exquisite, pearly-skinned, shiny-tailed creature.

Helga gave a very Sofie-like shrug. 'I make these things,' she said. 'It's what I do. Mostly, what I make, I sell. But this mermaid is for you, because you believe in them.'

Miranda was *that* close to tears. But then the café door opened again. This time it was Jack and Mrs Lovelace.

Mrs Lovelace smiled at the Happy Dazes racketing around, spilling juice and cake crumbs and giggling at the décor. 'Well I never!' she cried. 'And I thought we'd be the only ones here.' Then there were more cries of delight as she spotted Helga, whose ceramic figurines were famous, it seemed.

'I've spent hours in her china shop!' Mrs Lovelace informed them. But not with a shopping trolley, Miranda hoped.

'Watch them kids!' warned Jack, gruff as usual. So Miranda wrapped the ceramic mermaid up again before any little Happy Daze fingers could get to it.

The totally cool thing about both Mrs Lovelace and Helga was that they saw just as much beauty in the papier mâché mermaid. Even Jack said it was a ripper. And that got the Happy Dazes even more wound up.

'Well, I don't know,' Mrs Lovelace said. 'All these clever people make my little effort seem a bit feeble.'

Jack pulled her little effort from a shopping bag. It was a fabulous patchwork wall-hanging of a mermaid, with shells and seahorses all round the border.

'It was one way to fill in a rainy weekend,' Mrs Lovelace explained. 'And I had a bagful of bits.'

As Miranda hugged Mrs Lovelace, she could already imagine the mermaid hanging on her bedroom wall at home. It would be the bay and the sunshine and everything that had happened this summer, and they would stay with her through all the winter days.

Then Jack pulled something else out of the bag. It was a funny-shaped parcel bundled up in newspaper. He held it out to Miranda.

'The other one's for everybody,' he said. 'This one's for you.'

It was the merrow on her rock. Jack had carved her out of the same warm brown wood and polished her like an apple. But this time she was just the right size for Miranda to hold in her hands.

Everything was starting to be so fantastic that Miranda could feel herself turning to jelly. She needed some extra special words, and she couldn't find them. But she knew Jack wouldn't mind about that.

Blossom, with her hat over one eye, fought her way through Happy Dazes and put her arm around Miranda.

'It's Mermaid Monday in Mariners Bay,' she whispered, and she looked as blown away by it as Miranda felt.

And Blossom was exactly right. This was what it was all about. When Angus wrote about her mermaid dreaming, Miranda thought he was telling the world she was a total weirdo. But now all these people wanted to make the dreaming come true. This was a very different kind of magic, and it wouldn't save the Cosmos Café, but it was still utterly unreal and out of this world.

The minders gathered up their Dazes and said it was time they were going, so Miranda and Blossom walked them up to the car park. As their bus drove off, nearly as noisily as the Barneys', Angus's green beetle arrived.

By this time nothing was too surprising. So the pair of them only blinked very slightly when Captain Hornpipe leaped out, in full nineteenth-century sea captain's gear.

At least, that's who he said he was. This bizarre character was a cross between Long John Silver and Mr Bean. He kept cackling 'Heave-ho, me hearties!', swigging from a rum bottle and squinting at them through his spyglass. Miranda couldn't help thinking that any mermaid who fell in love with him would have to have rocks in her head.

It actually didn't take them long to work out that under the three-cornered hat and curly black beard was Bloom of the *Bugle* being seriously silly.

He made a big thing of clearing his throat, placed his hand over his heart, and in a not-bad baritone began to sing:

'Who pulled the plug on the mermaids?
What made the mermaids disappear?
Why did the mermaids turn up their tails and say,

"Adios! We're out of here!"?

'Oh, sweet Miranda, on her veranda,
Sits and gazes out across the bay.
Yes, sweet Miranda, on her veranda,
Dreaming dreams of mermaids every day.

'That's how it is with mermaids.
That's the way a mermaid tends to feel.
Somebody, somewhere, must believe in her,
Before a mermaid can get real.

'So, sweet Miranda, on your veranda,
All your mermaid dreaming hasn't been in vain.
Once there were mermaids here, Miranda.
And now there are mermaids again.

'Oh yeah!'

With that, Captain Hornpipe gave his spyglass a shake and from it a poster unfurled like a scroll.

It was a picture of a mermaid, a really big, bouncy, sexy one, with one eye closed in a cheeky wink. Her hair was like Blossom's, only more so, with crazy corkscrew curls sprouting everywhere. She hadn't bothered with a bra, either. Probably because she'd never have found seashells to fit her.

Blossom gave a hoot and fell about laughing, so Miranda knew it was OK for her to laugh too.

They were still laughing when Nygel, on his bike, threw a dirty great wheelie into the car park. He took one look at the mermaid and nearly fell off. That was nothing new, but the expression on his face made Blossom laugh so much that a couple of buttons pinged off her mauve gown.

In the end everybody got themselves sorted out and Angus told them that the poster was a gift from a cartoonist friend of his who had read the mermaid story in the *Bugle*.

'But I wrote the song myself,' he assured them.

What could they do but invite him down for a cuppa?

Nygel's backpack was stuffed with mail. It was all for Miranda Hodge, care of the Cosmos Café. Sofie had run out of pigeonholes and had told Nygel to get on his bike and deliver it to Miranda before they were buried under it.

Back at the café, Helga and Mrs Lovelace were washing up after the Happy Dazes and Jack was buttering himself a couple of mermaid muffins.

Nygel emptied his backpack onto a table. For Miranda it was like every Christmas and birthday she'd ever had rolled into one, except that all these envelopes and packages were from people she'd never even met. They'd sent handmade mermaid greetings cards, mermaid bookmarks, mermaid poems, mermaid stories, mermaid pictures and a whole heap of mermaid letters that would take her a week to read.

'I can't *believe* this!' she said. It was like the night they'd found Jack's merrow on the beach. So wonderful that she couldn't stop the tears from welling up.

And Mermaid Monday wasn't over yet.

Chapter 22

At half past eleven Zeus and Zephyr arrived, not only with Running Water, but with George as well.

Zephyr flipped the sign on the door to 'Open'. 'We passed the Barneys' bus along the road,' she announced. 'And that takes a bit of doing.'

'They're heading this way like they're hungry,' said George.

The sight of her former staff was too much for Blossom. She sat down with a bump at the Gemini table and burst into tears.

'Can't you do that later?' Zephyr asked. 'Right now we need to get cracking in the kitchen.' Suddenly she thought of something else. 'Hang on! Pressies! Where are the pressies, Zoo?'

Zeus plonked a paper parcel down in front of Blossom. She howled that she couldn't handle it, so Miranda opened it for her.

Zephyr had dyed some cheesecloth sea blue. She'd hand-printed it with mermaids swimming among shoals of fish and bubbles, and made it into a pair of sarongs. One for Blossom and one for Miranda. And Zeus had made them a tape of 'Song for Marina'.

'This is crazy.' Blossom wiped her eyes and straightened her hat. 'The whole world's gone crazy.'

Angus said it was the kind of craziness the world needed and there should be more of it.

And very shortly there was.

Within minutes the busload of Barneys rocked in, cheerful and rowdy as ever. The only one of them who was ever the slightest bit shy was the mum who'd run the Childcare Centre at the protest rally. And she was the one who was eagerly pushed forward now.

Rosy-faced, she handed Miranda a knitted doll. 'Just an idea I had,' she said.

Somebody else put in that it was more like divine inspiration.

But wherever the doll had come from, it was a gorgeous woolly mermaid with curves as cuddly as the one on the poster. Running Water took one look at her and fell madly in love. So he was allowed to keep her, and Miranda was promised another.

But that wasn't all. The Barneys had also come up with a set of china plates painted with something a bit different: mermaid angels.

'We're sure there are such things,' Miranda was told. 'We

really don't know who we're going to meet in heaven, do we?'

Then the ancient Barney beckoned Miranda over to his chair.

He took her hand in his bony, shaky one and looked at her with faded, watery eyes that were full of something important.

'My gran seen 'em,' he said. 'She seen them mermaids in the bay when she were a girl. She used to tell me about 'em when I was just a little bloke. Folks used to think she were spinning a yarn, but I knew it were true.'

He gave Miranda a very old creased brown-and-yellow photograph. Miranda gazed at the serious face of a young woman with scraped-back crinkly hair and a lacy collar fastened with a brooch high under her chin. She was staring straight out of the photo, and Miranda looked for a long time into eyes that had seen mermaids.

'You can keep that picture,' the old man said. Miranda didn't think she should, and tried to explain that they could have a copy made, but he wasn't having a bar of that.

'You're the one as should have it,' he said.

And that was a really great honour.

Miranda took the photograph down to her bedroom and tucked it into the corner of her dressing-table mirror. It was a pretty ordinary face, really, but so was her own. It just went to show that you didn't have to have a face like Rhiannon Fayn's to know about magical things.

Then she went back to the café to see what the rest of the day would bring.

It brought quite a lot. There was the shaggy-haired, round little man with the spirit of Pooh Bear who'd made her a stained-glass mermaid to hang in her window. Then there was the skinhead bikie in black with all the chains and tattoos. They thought he'd come looking for Nygel, but actually he'd done Miranda a mermaid picture in cross-stitch. It took Nygel a long time to get over that.

Cars kept rolling up and people kept coming in. They wanted to see thirteen-year-old Miranda Hodge. They wanted to see the bay where the ship was wrecked. Angus pointed out the exact spot where she went down, even though he hadn't a clue where it was.

People took photographs of the merrow on her rock and photographs of the swans. But the main thing they wanted to do was eat at the Cosmos Café. Blossom and Zephyr were flat out baking mermaid scones. Helga turned out to be a brilliant waitress. Zeus played his guitar and sang until his fingers nearly fell off and his voice went croaky. Then Angus took over and sang really silly mermaid songs that he made up as he went along. Later on he and Zeus talked about raising the money to make their own CD. It was that kind of a day.

By five o'clock it was all over. Everyone had gone, the

cleaning up had been done, and Miranda, Blossom and Nygel were sitting in beach chairs on the veranda. Miranda and Blossom were just lying back and letting memories of the day wash over them. Nygel was still brooding about the cross-stitching bikie.

Then, just like that, Blossom burst out, 'I can't leave this place! I can't!'

Miranda knew what she meant. Today had been unreal. But it was just one day, and there were years and years ahead. And it mattered so much to both of them that Blossom and the Cosmos should stay right here with these people where they belonged. And where Miranda belonged, too, whenever she could be here.

All of a sudden Nygel turned from a broody emu into a spotter dog. Muscles tensed, eyes riveted, he stared along the beach. Miranda could have sworn that his ears actually pricked forward and his nose quivered.

They looked where he was looking and saw a couple of loonies clowning around on the shoreline. They both had long legs and short shorts and they were leaping about, chasing each other in and out of the water, and laughing like maniacs.

Blossom peered over the top of her sunnies. 'It isn't, is it?' she gasped.

'It is, you know,' said Miranda. 'It's Christabel and her mum.'

No wonder Nygel had gone all aquiver. And no wonder Blossom couldn't believe her eyes.

The magic had been at it again, and this time it had zapped Weeping Willow. The hair she used to hide behind was up in a ponytail and she was all pink-faced and as silly as a circus as she sprinted towards them.

Christabel, once famous for her blank stares and stammer, came pelting behind her, even pinker and gigglier. It was quite awesome, really. And about to get more awesome still.

Willow wriggled her arms out of a backpack and tossed it onto the veranda. 'Hey!' she said brightly. 'We've come to see you!'

Blossom said she was really glad they had.

'Sorry to be so long,' Christabel told Miranda. 'But we've been doing heaps of stuff.'

Nygel just sat there with a dumb expression that didn't do a thing for his image.

Then Christabel remembered her manners and said, 'Mummy, I don't think you've met Nygel.'

Willow gave Nygel a smile that made all the blood rush to his face. 'Oh, but I have,' she said. 'You won't remember me, Nygel, because you were only little at the time. But I once designed a Celtic necklace and brooch for your mother. I had dinner at your house and Sofie brought you in to say goodnight.

I remember thinking what a sweetie you were in your little teddybear jamies.'

Miranda held her breath and waited for a really savage Mangler scowl, but it didn't happen. She couldn't think of a word that exactly described Nygel's expression, but 'simper' came close.

'See!' Blossom blurted before she could stop herself. 'I knew you were Willow Hampton!'

Willow shrugged, and smiled again. 'Any chance of a cuppa?' she asked, picking up her backpack. 'It's a long way from our place to yours. Or it is over those rocks, anyway.'

So they all went inside and Blossom dashed off to make a pot of comfrey tea. She even found a jug of orange juice that the Happy Dazes had missed, and the last batch of mermaid scones.

Miranda could feel that there was something going on with Willow and Christabel. They weren't just here for a friendly visit. There was something else. It was something zingy and electric, excited and exciting.

They were both knocked out by all the mermaids around the place. 'Unreal!' sighed Christabel. 'Wicked!' her mother agreed. And the excitement level zoomed even higher. Miranda was busting to know what it was all about.

She didn't have long to wait. Once they were all sitting

round the Taurus table, Christabel looked at Willow and said, 'Well, go on!'

Willow rolled her eyes and said, 'O . . . K!' the way you do when you've got something ultra-important to say.

'First up,' she said, 'I have to tell you that we're staying. We got an email from Jerome's solicitor, and Jerome is giving the house to Christabel. I'm the trustee until she's eighteen.'

Miranda gulped, Blossom gaped, and Nygel missed his mouth with a muffin.

'Cool, eh?' said Christabel. 'We're moving down here right away. Mummy loves it here. It's a magical place.'

Miranda wondered why it had taken them so long to work that out. But it was the look on Blossom's face that she cared about most. Blossom was doing her best to look thrilled for Willow and Christabel. But her eyes were saying, *So easy for you, and so tough for me!*

Now Willow was talking again. 'We've got plans,' she said. 'We're going to restore the house and the gardens. Not change them, just make them as beautiful as they once were.' Then she looked Blossom full in the face. 'But that's not all. This place, your amazing things in the living room, the mermaid dreaming, those fabulous mermaids in your studio, they got me thinking.'

She opened her backpack and pulled out a sketchbook. 'More than thinking, they got me *doing*. I'll show you.'

170

They all leaned forward to look, even Nygel.

Willow had done lots of ink and watercolour sketches of jewellery. Mermaid jewellery. And even like that, just sketches on paper, Miranda could see what it was that made Willow Hampton jewellery so special.

Slender mermaids with flowing hair wove their way in an underwater ballet around a silver bangle. The pendant hanging on a chain of tiny seashells was a mermaid sitting on an anchor like a child on a swing. Mermaids twirled on earring trapezes and curled themselves into rings for fingers and toes. There were mermaid hairclips, mermaid brooches, mermaid hatpins and clasps. Just looking at them sent Miranda floating off into another world.

'This wouldn't be expensive stuff,' Willow was explaining. 'It'd be fun stuff that people can afford. Fun! I haven't had any of that in a long time. But I'm going to have some now!' She waved her arm around the café at all the other creations that Mermaid Monday had brought. 'Look at this lot. Doesn't it prove I'm right?' Suddenly she reached out and grabbed Blossom's hand. 'Trust me, Blossom! We can do this thing!'

Blossom was doing a pretty good imitation of Nygel doing an imitation of a gobsmacked goldfish. And Miranda knew what was spinning her out. Did 'we' mean 'we' as in Blossom and Willow? And what thing was it that they could do?

In the end it was Christabel who brought her mother back to earth.

'You haven't told them yet,' she said. 'Go on, tell them.'

So Willow did.

'A gallery!' she cried. 'We're going to turn that whopping great dining room that we'd never use into an arts and crafts gallery.'

'Not any old arts and crafts,' Christabel chimed in. 'Only things that belong here. Things that . . . that . . .' She couldn't quite say what she meant, so Miranda said it for her. 'Things that have the spirit of the bay.'

'Right,' said Christabel. 'The spirit.'

Blossom was slowly turning the pages of the sketchbook. 'There'd be your jewellery here in the bay?' It seemed too utterly amazing for her to get her head around.

'Right here in this café,' said Willow. 'We could have it in both places. Not just jewellery, but the gorgeous stuff you make and all these other people make. We can work together and have a gallery, and a café, and a gift shop. What d'you say?'

For a long time nobody said anything. Then Nygel squared his scrawny shoulders and came out with, 'Yeah, cool. Why not?'

And for once Nygel had got it right.

'Yes!' cried Blossom. 'Why not?'

Chapter 28

Miranda slowly folded her new sarong and put it in the top of the dreaded pink plastic suitcase. She was almost at the end of her packing and she was doing it by herself. Christabel had offered to help, but Miranda needed to be alone. There was just so much going on in her head.

This afternoon she would be on a plane to Sydney. Nygel was flying home to Melbourne tomorrow. It was like reading the last page of a Rhiannon Fayn novel. She knew that it had to end, but she wished it didn't have to be quite yet.

For the first time since the day she'd arrived she was wearing her jeans. Only now she could get both hands inside the waistband, and her blouse buttoned up without gaping or pulling tight underneath her arms.

Most of her goodbyes had already been said. Willow and Christabel had given her and Nygel a farewell party in their new home last night. They'd invited everyone they knew: Zephyr,

Zeus and Running Water; Sofie, Jack and Mrs Lovelace, all the Barneys, Angus . . . so many people she'd known for only a few weeks, but seemed to have known all her life.

The house had still reminded Miranda of a gracious old lady, but now she was awake and welcoming. Even Jerome's ritzy modern furniture, which Willow hadn't had a chance to change yet, couldn't take away the genteel charm of the tall ceilings and windows and the mellow polished wood panelling.

Willow was right. The spirit of the house and the views across the bay made the perfect setting for a gallery. And Willow had experience and good taste and knew how to run a business. Jerome and his Thrillboats had been totally wrong for the bay. But Willow and Blossom could make things happen that were exactly right.

So Miranda and Nygel were going, and Christabel was staying. Christabel, who could have anything she wanted, was now going to have the bay. She was going to travel to Hobart on the school bus and come home every afternoon to that fabulous house. It was a writer's dream house, and Christabel wasn't a writer. But it was Christabel who would sit by a log fire and listen to wild winter storms and the thunder of waves; Christabel who would walk on the beach in the mist and the rain. She would know the bay in all its seasons and moods.

That was cool. Somehow Miranda didn't feel jealous. Maybe

that was because Willow had told Blossom her story, and Blossom had told Miranda.

Jerome, a true Ambrazine, could suss out money the way a blowfly could suss out a barbecue (Blossom's words, not Willow's). That was why he had targeted Willow when he was looking for wife number four.

Willow's jewellery design business was small, but very exclusive and very successful. She kept herself out of the lime-light and only did the things that she really wanted to do. What Jerome didn't understand was that she liked it that way. Maybe he thought she was too dumb to aim for the big time.

As soon as they were married he was in her ear about ways to get seriously rich and famous. He had trouble believing her when she said she didn't want to be either.

When Christabel was born, Willow wanted to pull back even further. Jerome had enough money for all three of them, and she was more interested in being a mum than making mega-bucks. But for Jerome there was never enough money. He hung around for a few more years, just to make sure that he wasn't going to miss out if Willow changed her mind. Then he dumped her for a nineteen-year-old heiress who'd just inherited a stable full of racehorses.

'That just wiped the poor woman out,' Blossom told Miranda. 'She went totally *clunk*, and turned into Weeping Willow.'

Miranda could see that it must have been really awful for Christabel, too. No wonder she ended up with a zombie stare and a stammer. But Mariners Bay had fixed all that, and everything was looking great.

Now Miranda was leaving. It was time to say goodbye to her room. She closed her suitcase and sat down beside it on the bed, remembering that first day when she'd sat there wrapped in a towel because she didn't know what else to do. Since then Miranda and this room had become part of each other.

One thing she was really glad about. The room wouldn't stay empty and silent after she'd gone. Angus was going to use it as his office while he wrote his book.

It felt good to know that, any time she wanted to, she could imagine him there. She could already see him sitting at his desk in the corner with his bits of paper and his books, peering through his glasses at his notes and tapping away at his word processor. Angus would keep this little room alive and needed until she came back to it again.

Miranda picked up her suitcase and went out into the café. She had to stop thinking of it as the Cosmos. Now it was the Mermaid Café and Gift Shop. Or it would be when a whole mob of people had finished with it.

Blossom and Willow were up on trestles painting a brilliant sea blue over the eyeball, the fish and the flowering belly button. Jack was varnishing a showcase he'd built all along one wall. Zeus and Angus, with some help from Running Water, were trying out songs for their CD, and Mrs Lovelace was cutting out curtains that matched the mermaid sarongs.

At the Pisces table, Christabel was designing a mural to go on the walls. And at the Taurus table, Zephyr was working out a new menu.

It was Willow who'd been brave enough to suggest that last one. 'People sometimes do like a cup of tea that's actually got tea in it,' she'd said. 'Even a coffee made from coffee beans. And when they're on holiday and feel like being really wicked, they might even want cake with chocolate in it instead of seaweed.'

When she'd seen the look on Blossom's face, she'd said, 'Trust me! By the time they've climbed back up to the car park, they'll have worked off all the sinful stuff.'

It was a tough decision. But in the end the staff had agreed that perhaps they didn't have to be organic *all* the time.

Blossom looked round at Miranda, then looked at her watch and jumped down from the trestle.

'Yeah, it's time,' she said. 'I want to call at the post office on the way, so we'd better get going.'

She dashed off to change out of her painting smock, and it was time for Miranda to say her goodbyes again. Both she and

Christabel got a bit wussy, and Christabel's eyes were swimming with tears.

'Will you come back at Easter?' she asked.

Miranda didn't know. How could she afford the airfare?

Christabel must have read her thoughts. 'My mother'll pay,' she said.

But Miranda wasn't sure what Brian and Judy would think about that, so all she could say was, 'We'll see.'

They all wanted to troop up to the car park to see her off, but Miranda asked them not to. Jack said he'd carry her suitcase up. Then he said, 'In a minute,' and she knew that was because he understood.

She'd never been able to walk straight through the garden. And she certainly wasn't going to this last time. She wandered slowly and breathed in its smells and the feeling she always had that this garden was somehow outside of time and place, and that something of Theodelinda lingered there.

Then she climbed up the steep path. The Kombi was unlocked, but she didn't get in. Instead she stood and looked down at the roof of the café. It was still blue and still covered with giant butterflies. And Blossom had promised it would stay that way.

In the last moments she had all to herself, she gazed out across the bay. The distant hills were hazy, but the sea was a sparkling patchwork of green and turquoise and blue. Today there was a bit of a breeze rippling the water. Where the sun hit the ripples it made dazzling flashes, like a bright light hitting glass.

It was while she was staring at the ripples and the flashes that Miranda thought she just might have glimpsed something else. Did she see shapes moving in the water? The gleam of a sleek wet head? The shimmer of a waving arm? The glint of a shining tail?

Then she became aware of Jack plodding up the slope with her suitcase. Behind him was Blossom, in a clean muslin shirt, but with blue paint still on her nose and in her hair. And when Miranda looked out to sea again, all that was there were the swans.

Jack shoved Miranda's case into the back of the Kombi, and then fixed her with his fierce glare. 'Just you come back soon!' he growled. And Miranda promised to do her best.

Blossom could have filled in the drive to the post office with lots of chatting, but she didn't. All she said was, 'Without you, Mim, none of this would have happened.' Then she left Miranda to gaze out of the window and think her own thoughts.

But if Miranda had thoughts that she wanted to keep to herself, Sofie had plenty that she wanted to offload.

With Nygel's hair just long enough to start to curl and his

179

new tooth installed, she was sending him home in pretty much as good condition as he'd arrived, except that he was missing three socks, a bedroom slipper and a handmade genuine silk shirt (Miranda seemed to remember him cleaning his bike with that).

Nygel himself was slouched against the catfood, scowling into his motorbike magazine and trying out his new tooth on his fingernails.

Miranda knew he was only doing that because she was standing there in her going-home clothes. But he was going to have to say something to her sooner or later. So when Sofie and Blossom went off to check the mail, she stayed where she was and waited.

'Well,' she said, just to get a conversation started, 'I'm off today.'

'You're off every day,' he shot back with his usual razor-sharp wit.

What else could she expect from Nygel? But she certainly wasn't expecting what she got next.

From somewhere among the Tiddles Tuna Treats he pulled out a fat paperback book and thrust it at her.

'There you go,' he said, giving her one of his most menacing Mangler snarls.

Miranda looked at the book. On the front cover was a

picture of a gorgeous but pretty uptight looking girl in medieval clothes. She was being dive-bombed by a bunch of black crows and didn't seem happy about it.

The Curse of the Wyldewood Ravens, Miranda read. *Volume Five of the Tressellyn Chronicles*, by Rhiannon Fayn.

While she was still trying to get her head around that, Nygel grunted, 'Look inside.'

She turned to the first page, and her heart flipped. The most beautiful bookplate had been glued there. It was decorated with a border of Celtic knots, and in golden ink and flowing Celtic script was written, *To Dear Miranda, with my warmest wishes*, and then the famous signature *Rhiannon Fayn*.

Miranda read the bookplate three times. Then she stared at Nygel. He was still wearing his Mangler face, but when he spoke his voice no longer sounded as though she was top of his hit list.

'I got her to send it,' he said. 'It's an advance copy. That means it's not in the shops yet.'

'Thanks.'

'It's OK.' He shrugged. 'You can show it to that Jacques person if you want. That should pee her off big time.'

Miranda said she was sure it would. Then Nygel went back to slouching and she just stood there.

'Right,' she said at last. 'Well. See you, Nygel with a Y, and good luck with your streetfighting.'

Nygel actually cracked a smile. 'See ya, Highness,' he said. 'And next time, we're dreaming up those dead guys, OK?'

Saying goodbye to Sofie was just as Miranda expected. The goddess's feelings were all over the place.

'Today you, tomorrow Nygel,' she cried. 'It breaks my heart! What shall we do without you?' She grabbed Miranda by her shoulders and kissed her on both cheeks. 'Don't forget us, dear Miranda. Come back to us as soon as you can!' And she gave her a Special Gift Pack of Hughey McDewey's Super Chewy Toffees to eat on the plane.

Up until then Miranda had been hanging together quite well. But with Sofie in tears, she was close to losing it herself. And she wasn't about to let that happen in front of Nygel.

'Will you come back at Easter?' he called as she groped her way out of the door.

'Dunno,' she yelled back, and dived into the Kombi before he could say that his mother would pay.

As Blossom drove off, Miranda looked in the mirror. The last she saw of Mariners Bay was the dead dog chasing them down the empty street.

Theodelinda was going home. Part of her heart she was leaving behind in an alien land that had become so dear. But already her thoughts were racing ahead to her own land and her own beloved, loyal and devoted people.

At last, at last, the long journey was over. She could see them gathered there to greet her, and hear their joyous, welcoming cries.

'Far out! Look at her!'

'Her bum's only half the size it was!'

'Yoohoo, sweetheart! Over here!'

It was Kelly she saw first. How could she miss her in a hat the size of a garbage bin lid and a boofy lace dress that looked like a three-tiered wedding cake?

And there was Brian, an over-the-moon grin on his sun-tanned face, and still in overalls, as though he'd come straight from HoHoing somewhere. And then she was wrapped in a Judy hug that was like falling into a feather mattress.

Miranda was going home. Home to cold chocolate milk with ice cream on top. Home to mangy dogs and piddling cats that only needed love. Home to a room with cracks in the ceiling and biro stains on the doona, a room that she shared with a Celtic Warrior Princess.

Dear Tallulah Hopewell (Ms),

Thank you for writing to tell me that you do not exist. And thank you for telling me that you are really Miranda Hodge. Somehow I had a feeling that you might be.

Miranda, I very much agree with your decision to withdraw your story from our competition on the grounds that it might hurt some people's feelings. I have no desire to be sued by every member of the Ambrazine family. Or by any of the Jacques family for that matter. And I especially do not want to be sued by Rhiannon Fayn.

Also, had you completed an entry form, you might have noticed that stories were to be not more than 3,000 words in length. So I would have had to disqualify you anyway.

Having said all that, I want you to know that I enjoyed your story immensely. You are a remarkably gifted writer

for your age, and I'm sure that in a few years' time
Rhiannon Fayn will have to start watching her back.

May I also say that you are an exceptional person.
And exceptional people do sometimes get dumped on, so
don't let it worry you. Hang in there and keep writing.

Yours very sincerely,
Hughey McDewey (Mr)